THE GREAT GALLOON

Bean Primary School
School Lane
Bean, Dartford
Kent DA2 8AL

THE GREAT GALLOON

Being a mostly accurate
tale of the voyages of
Captain Meredith Anstruther,
his crew and his celebrated
Great Galloon.

TOM BANKS

HOT
KEY
BOOKS

First published in Great Britain in 2013 by Hot Key Books
Northburgh House, 10 Northburgh Street, London EC1V 0AT

A CIP catalogue record for this book is available from the British Library.

ISBN: 978-1-4714-0088-9

1

Typeset by Palimpsest Book Production Limited, Falkirk, Stirlingshire
This book is set in 11.75 pt Sabon LT Std

Printed and bound by Clays Ltd, St Ives Plc

FSC

Hot Key Books supports the Forest Stewardship Council (FSC), the leading
international forest certification organisation, and is committed to printing
only on Greenpeace-approved FSC-certified paper.

www.hotkeybooks.com

Hot Key Books is part of the Bonnier Publishing Group
www.bonnierpublishing.com

For Dulcie, Sol and Sarah,
and for Nell.
The real Team GB x

Dear Reader,

Throughout these stories of 'The Great Galloon' you will find goodnight points. Please be aware that these are the author's suggestion only. If you are reading this story to your brother, vicar, fridge, etc, please feel free to move goodnight points around exactly as you see fit. If you are reading this story to yourself, you may, of course, ignore the goodnight points altogether and carry on reading forever, until the story ends, or you walk into a lamppost, whichever happens first.

The Bilgepumps on the Great Galloon

The Great Galloon creaked and snapped as it pulled at its anchors, thousands of feet above the frozen sea. Its sails were furled; its great boiler pumped hot air into the gigantic balloon that kept it in the sky, and onboard was a flurry of activity such as Stanley Crumplehorn had never seen before.

Rushing along the decks, on his way from his own cabin to the ballroom, he ducked as a walking stick flew through the air an inch from his head.

'Sorry, dear!' cried Mrs Wouldbegood, the wizened and wrinkly owner of the stick, who was fighting off a bearded man with a cutlass.

'No problem,' called Stanley, as he leapt down a low flight of stairs that led to the main deck. A box of crockery came smashing to the ground as he passed and Stanley heard Mrs Wouldbegood roaring, 'That's

1

the best dinner service, you piratical dog!' before he dropped down a hatchway and into the relative darkness of the wooden corridor below. As he landed on the boards, he heard a clattering behind him. He turned to look down the wide passageway, and saw a tangle of wheels and tongues hurtling towards him. It was a small cart, being pulled by four big, slobbery hounds, and driven by the stripy-jumpered cabin boy, Clamdigger. He was grasping the reins in one hand, while flapping the other at a scruffy-looking man behind him. Stanley jumped to one side and pressed himself against the wall. As the panting dogs passed him, he stuck out an arm just in time for Clamdigger to grab it with his spare hand and haul Stanley aboard.

'Heading for the officers' mess?' called Clamdigger, over the sounds of slavering and panting, and the cursing of his would-be assailant.

'Just as far as the ballroom,' said Stanley, desperately trying to keep upright the large vase of flowers he was carrying, while avoiding the fracas. 'How are things going, do you think?' Stanley called out.

'Fine, fine. Nearly finished the decorations, and Ms Huntley has made all her preparations. Should go off without a hitch, as long as the best man arrives on time.' He said all this while driving expertly and keeping the scruffy man at arm's length.

'The best man?' asked Stanley, looking up at the gangly boy.

'Yes – the Captain's brother. He's on his way right now.'

As Clamdigger said this, the filthy man who had been trying to throttle him gave a startled cry. He let go of Clamdigger's throat and leapt from the back of the cart, crying, 'There's two of 'em! We're undone, lads!!' as he rolled along the wooden floor.

'He doesn't seem too pleased,' said Stanley, smiling, as Clamdigger brought the cart to a skittering halt.

'Who?' said the boy, settling the dogs with a reassuring pat.

'That man who was trying to throttle you,' said Stanley, pointing at the man running back the way he had come.

'Serves him right, I suppose. Although you can't help feeling sorry for them, with both the Captain and his brother to deal with. Anyway – here we are. The ballroom. See you later, Stanley.' With a flick of the reins and a yelp from the hounds, Clamdigger continued on his way.

Stanley watched him go, then turned to face a pair of high wooden doors, inlaid with iron. With a sense of relish, he pushed them open.

The scene was like a cross between a ballet and a riot. Far away, at the other end of the Galloon's gigantic

ballroom, he could see a band of white-coa[t]
duelling with a group of ruffians, while sim
laying the tables. In the middle of the roor
top of a teetering stepladder was cleaning a chandelier
while avoiding the blows of a huge hammer, wielded
by a troll-like creature. As Stanley watched, the monster's
weapon made contact with the chandelier itself,
dislodging a precious crystal, which dropped towards
the floor. But far below, a woman in leather trousers
and a cocked hat put out a hand at precisely the correct
moment to catch the crystal, without so much as looking
up from the book she was reading.

'Do you take this lady, Isabella Croucher, to be your
lawful . . .' she read, as she flung the crystal back into
the air. Up the ladder, the cleaner caught it effortlessly,
flicked his ladder around on its axis, and sent the troll
sliding across the dancefloor, where it came to rest in
a pile of gold-coloured chairs.

'Thank you, Ms Huntley!' cried the cleaner, at which
the leather-clad lady raised a calm hand and carried
on reading to herself.

'I, Navigator Huntley, by the power vested in me
by you, my Captain and friend, declare you man and
wife . . .' she muttered, and carried on pacing.

Stanley set off across the floor, jinking to avoid flying
furniture, as he made his way towards the distant top
table. Despite the chaos going on all around, things

ere getting done. The tables were laid, and an army of sweepers was crossing the hall to and fro, gathering up indignant marauders along with the dust and debris. The chairs were being laid out by a human chain, which neatly flung each one over the heads of the attackers as if they weren't even there.

Stanley could see the raiders were getting more and more frustrated, partly at their lack of success, and partly at the nonchalant way they were being fought off – as if they were no more irritating than a swarm of midges. Stanley stopped as a man swinging a curved sword stepped backwards across his tracks. The man was grunting and sweating with the effort of holding off a smartly clad butler, who himself was entirely unruffled.

The butler was using a chair to push the swordsman backwards, while calmly dictating to his assistant. 'And then we shall need the choir to be ready as the Captain and his bride walk back up the aisle . . . Oh, look, another chair ruined.'

Seeming finally to notice the fuming swordsman, the butler said sternly, 'This just isn't on! We have barely enough chairs for guests as it is. Now, *please* . . .'

He flung the shattered chair away.

'Be . . .'

He picked the man up and held him aloft on one arm as if he were a tray of teacups.

'More . . .'

He spun the man round and round.

'Careful!'

And he flung him almost carelessly away, where he landed with an 'Oof' on the unconscious troll-like creature, who hugged him close and began to suck his topknot like a dummy.

'Now,' said the butler, 'young Stanley Crumplehorn, please get a move on. Those flowers should be on the top table by now. Stop gawping, boy, scurry on!'

Stanley didn't mind being spoken to like this by Snivens the butler, who was a kindly man at heart, so he merely tugged his forelock and began to run again. Now he was nearing the top table, where a group of people was huddled together as if discussing something important. An arm flew out of the huddle and grabbed one of the invaders by the hair. It twisted him round like a clockwork toy, and a different person's leg gave him a kick up the backside, which sent him tottering away with a howl. Stanley laughed, which caused the huddle to break up. The first person to turn to Stanley was a tall, beautiful woman with kindly eyes and a glitzy tiara.

'Aha! The flowers,' said the Dowager Countess of Hammerstein, bending down to Stanley's height. 'Thank you, Stanley, my darling. I thought for a moment we were going to have a crisis on our hands!'

Saying this, she put out an elegant foot and sent a brutish-looking man tumbling under a table. She took the flowers from Stanley's hands and handed them to a pale girl in a purple dress.

'On the top table, I think, Cloudier, dear,' said the Countess.

'Yes'm,' said Cloudier, moving away with the flowers. She pulled them out of the vase, which she threw towards a wild-looking woman brandishing a cutlass. Confused, the woman threw out both arms to catch the vase, causing her to drop the cutlass on her foot.

Cloudier winked at Stanley, causing him to blush, which only made him blush harder.

As the wild-looking woman hopped past, Stanley saw that the man in the middle of the huddle had been the man who all this fuss was for – the most important man onboard, the man who owned the whole Galloon, and on whom they all relied: Captain Meredith Anstruther.

'Well, Stanley!' said the Captain, effortlessly grasping a black-clad pirate in each enormous hand. 'What a day, eh? What a day! Makes the heart glad. Thank you for bringing the flowers; the Countess was beginning to worry!'

With this, he gave a sideways look to the glamorous woman now arranging the flowers on the table, who

8

rolled her eyes and smiled. The Captain seemed to forget what he was doing for a moment, then dropped the two pirates into a convenient dustbin and closed the lid.

'Now, young . . . err . . . man,' he said, with the merest glance at the short, blunt horn on Stanley's head. 'I hear word that my brother is approaching. Let us hail him at the boatswain's chair.'

'Yes, sir!' said Stanley quietly. Stanley was not usually one for calling people 'sir', but the Captain was different. He was physically enormous, with shoulders like a pair of upturned jollyboats, and a broad, red-brown face. He wore on his ponytailed head a hat that would have looked ridiculous on anybody else, but gave him an air of majesty. It was a dusty, black, three-cornered thing from a former age, with gold piping and a tail of black ribbon, which somehow made him look even more formidable. Stanley followed as the Captain turned and walked away.

'Ermm – Captain?' he called, realising immediately how weedy his voice sounded after the Captain's profound rumble. 'This isn't the way to the chair, is it? We have to go back through the . . .'

'Back through the ballroom, along the top corridor, up hatchway alpha fifteen, past the kennels, up the for'ard stairs, round the north bulwarks, over the ropings, under the foreb'loon capstans, and out past

9

the jakes. I know. That's the way to go alright – when you're not with *me*. But today, young man – you are!'

With this, the Captain looked around and gave a stealthy shove against a golden candelabra. With a creak that spoke of years of disuse, a door that had seemed to be part of the panelling opened up before them. As the Captain stepped inside, he beckoned for Stanley to do the same.

'Is it safe?' asked Stanley, before he could stop himself.

'Safe? Safe?' rumbled the Captain, as his eyes creased with laughter. 'I built this whole vessel with my own two hands, my boy! You'll trust it if you trust me!'

Immediately, Stanley squeezed inside the small space, feeling the Captain's massive presence, with his familiar smell of waxed cloth and chalk dust, as both reassuring and slightly overwhelming.

'Well. I am very pleased. Very pleased indeed,' said the Captain, looking down at Stanley from under his massive hat. Then, pausing only to slam the door shut on the necktie of a marauder who chose that moment to leap at them, the Captain pulled a lever that formed the back of the candelabra. The wooden floor of their little closet quivered, and then Stanley felt the blood rush from his face as it shot upwards, propelling them into the darkness.

He could hear the trundling of a mechanism, and

he could see the walls rattling by – this was obviously a secret route that only the Captain knew about. Later on Stanley would come back to the ballroom and examine that candelabra minutely, but never make it do anything other than hold a candle. For now though, he was simply enjoying the ride.

'Where does this lead to?' he said after a few moments.

'Up and out!' said the Captain, and he smiled a broad smile. In all his time onboard the Galloon, Stanley had never seen the Captain smile like this. His usual smiles, when they came at all, seemed to be more about being polite or making someone feel better, than about smiling because he couldn't help it. But now his wide face split in two as they raced together up the narrow chute.

Looking up, past the Captain, Stanley saw the top of the chute coming closer. He just had time to notice that it was covered by a wooden grill, before the Captain kicked out at another lever as they shot past. The grill opened just as they reached it, and Stanley and the Captain were popped out of the top of the chute like a cork from a bottle. Stanley gasped as the Captain gripped him tightly, and then felt his eyes water as the cold air hit.

They carried on flying up into the bright nothingness of a clear day, and as he looked down, Stanley saw

the deck of the Galloon stretched out beneath them. It was so big that he couldn't see the sea, thousands of feet below, but his stomach flipped nevertheless. Ropes and pulleys began to flit by. This was the network that connected the Galloon – a gigantic ship-like vessel the size of a city – to the balloon that kept it in the air, and the sails that allowed it to remain under the Captain's control. Stanley looked up and saw that the Captain was still smiling, but now with a slightly more manic look in his eye.

'Hold on,' he boomed. 'I'm going to need both hands!'

Still whistling upwards through the air, Stanley managed to hook both hands under the Captain's great shiny leather belt, and wrapped his feet around one thick boot.

'Good lad, Stanley! This is the life, eh?' yelled the Captain, and Stanley felt a thrill at the idea of sharing this adventure with such a man.

With his hands free, and with their weight now returning, the Captain reached out and grabbed one of the many ropes that hung nearby. They fell, as Stanley knew they must, but rather than straight down, they swung out and across the deck of the Galloon, towards the mighty main mast, twelve oak tree trunks lashed in a bundle, from which all the sails hung.

Before they slammed into it, however, the Captain

13

let go, and they were flying again. Then he grabbed another rope, and they began to fall straight down. Their fall was checked by a bucket flying upwards, a bucket which, Stanley just had time to notice, held two terrified-looking raiders. But he didn't have time to feel sorry for them in their plight, as the Captain, now growling like a bear, plucked Stanley out of his fall, and onto a frail-looking ladder. And frail it was, as the Captain's steel-capped boots smashed the rung they were on, then the one below that, and they fell again, crashing through the rungs in a fall barely controlled by the Captain clinging gamely onto the uprights, with hands that were soon emitting a faint burning smell.

'Nearly there!' were the Captain's strangled words as their descent began to slow and, daring to look down, Stanley saw the deck approaching at a rate that was almost slow enough not to kill them. With a last gasp of effort, the Captain threw out his arms, which flung the pair of them backwards off the ladder. Stanley's stomach flipped yet again as they flopped against the taut fabric of a sail, and slid slowly deck-wards. They dropped the last few feet, and the Captain's boots slammed solidly into the planks. There was a moment of pause, then Stanley unhooked his hands, took a step back, and looked up at the Captain. He was still beaming like a schoolboy, despite the smoke rising from the palms of his upturned hands.

14

'Thank you, sir,' said Stanley shakily.

'No, my lad. Thank you,' said the Captain. 'Most people try to stop me from doing things like that nowadays. Damned dull existence, being in charge.' And the Captain threw his head back and laughed like a drain. This was to be the last time Stanley would see him laugh for a very long time.

Their flight, their arrival, and the Captain's demonic appearance had not gone unnoticed. Across the decks, the boarders from the enemy vessel, whatever and wherever it was, were making a run for it. The crew of the Galloon was well used to events of this nature, and Stanley could see them already turning their full attention back to the wedding preparations.

'Hail there,' called the Captain to a knot of Gallooniers nearby. 'Any sign of my brother?'

'Aye, Cap'n,' said the nearest man, snapping to attention. 'Periscope spotted off the larboard quarter.'

'Good work, Sampson,' said the Captain. 'And none of this salutin' clart. We're not in the blessed navy.'

'Aye, sir. No, sir. Sorry, sir. I mean . . .'

But the man's words were lost as the Captain strode on, and Stanley trotted after him.

'D'you know where the larboard quarter is, lad?' said the Captain, staring out at the horizon.

'No, sir.'

'No. Neither do most right-thinking people, which

15

is why I know I can trust you to say 'over there' if that's what you mean.'

'Sir.'

As they talked, they approached the taffrail, which ran all the way around the deck, and which Stanley now knew to refer to as 'the rail that runs all round the deck'. The Captain looked over, and Stanley, being shorter by a good three feet or more, scrambled up onto a pile of crates to do the same.

'By Jove, that is quite a sight,' said the Captain between his teeth, and Stanley could only agree. Below the Galloon, thousands of feet beneath them, the sea was swarming with tiny vessels. A flotilla of mismatched boats was pulling, sailing, steaming, and chugging away from the Galloon as fast as possible, with more people joining the exodus by the moment. Defeated raiders were parachuting into the little boats, or abseiling into the sea, to be picked up by whichever rescuer came along next.

'Another raid successfully repelled, Captain,' said Stanley.

'What? Yes, yes, of course,' said the Captain. 'But they're two a penny. You can wish for a better class of raiders, but you won't get 'em. No – I'm referring to *that!*'

Stanley followed his finger, and saw that the sea was behaving strangely. Where the little boats had been rowing across a calm sea, they were now dealing with rolling waves where none should be – the sea was suddenly boiling and heaving like a pot of soup. Stanley watched one boat as it came to a standstill. The water it was sitting in, apparently thousands of feet deep just a moment before, suddenly became as shallow as a duck pond. Stanley realised that the whole seabed must be rising up to meet them – or at least the part of it that he was looking at, an area covering hundreds of feet in every direction.

As his eyes began to adjust to this change, he saw that it was true. The hull of a vessel, like an upturned bath on a massive scale, broke the water, and scattered many of the tiny boats in all directions. This new submarine ship wasn't anything like the size of the Galloon, but it was impressively big, in the same way that a whale is big until you compare one to a mountain. It seemed to be made of metal plates, patched and worn but immensely strong. As it surfaced, the Captain wiped his brow with his greasy red neckerchief.

'He's built it. Ha! Good for you, Zebediah. I knew it could be done,' he said and thumped the rail with an open hand.

Before Stanley could wonder what this meant, one of the panels on the new ship was pushed back like a hatchway, and out of it there clambered a man. He stood up uncertainly on the pitching hull, then raised a whistle to his lips. He blew three short blasts, a long note, and then one more short one.

'Means it's time for Abel to lower the chair,' said the Captain, and looked along the rail to where a group of crew members was forming itself efficiently into a welcoming party. Stanley recognised Clamdigger and a few others in the party, but he couldn't see the distinctive slender figure of Able Skyman Abel, the closest thing the Galloon had to an officer.

It seemed the Captain couldn't see him either, as he stood up and mumbled, 'Blast yer eyes, Abel. Where have you got to?'

'He couldn't have been . . . injured in the raid, sir?' said Stanley.

'What? Raid? No, no. Not if I'm any judge. He'll be around somewhere. Doing . . . you know. Duties. He likes duties.' The Captain scoured the deck with his eyes. It seemed to Stanley that he was willing Abel to appear.

'Clamdigger!' he called after a moment. 'You able to lower the chair?'

'Yes, sir. No problem,' called Clamdigger in reply.

'Then do so. And light along, can you? I've got a bride to wed.'

Saying this, he turned on his heel and walked towards the centre of the deck, just in front of the main mast, where a canopy had been set up, and two leather armchairs for the Captain and his brother to sit in.

Stanley followed along, unsure of what to do for the best. The Captain gestured to Stanley to sit in the left-hand chair, which gave Stanley another brief thrill. The Captain himself stood, however, and watched as Clamdigger efficiently organised the lowering of the boatswain's chair: a kind of hammock on a pulley system that was lowered over the side to allow people to enter and leave the Galloon.

Having seen the contraption go over the side, the Captain turned to sit in his own chair. But before doing so, he narrowed his eyes and squinted at it. Then he reached down, picked up one of the large golden cushions that covered it, and threw it to one side. Then he took a step back and pushed his hat up on his head, with a look of calm concern on his face. Stanley jumped up on his own chair, and peeped over into the other. There he saw that the Captain had uncovered a blue-clad bottom, attached to a thin pair of legs and two shiny black boots. Someone had apparently been hiding under the cushions.

'Abel?' said the Captain, with the same tone of calm concern as his face was showing. 'Abel?' he said again, louder. When this got no response, he took off his hat and used it to bat the bottom, as gently as was possible with such a solid thing. The bottom recoiled, and from behind another cushion appeared a long, pale face, with a white moustache and watery eyes. The face looked terrified at first, but when it saw the Captain it relaxed into a nervous grin.

'Abel,' said the Captain. 'You can come out now. The raid, such as it was, is over.'

'Aha! Captain, how lucky it is that you found me here . . .' said Abel, now rolling clumsily off the chair, and straightening his stick-like limbs until he stood before them.

'Yes, yes,' said the Captain, still seeming more concerned than annoyed. 'You weren't injured, I hope, in the raid?'

'No, no,' said Abel, looking sheepish (which is easy when your face is obscured by a woolly white moustache). 'Just, protecting the, er, the money, that one inevitably finds behind chair cushions . . .'

He rambled into silence as the Captain's face grew sterner.

'I don't like to think you weren't playing your part, Abel,' said the Captain, thoughtfully. 'Everyone can help at times like these, and that doesn't just mean fighting.'

'Ah, but sir, I thought it was important to . . .' Abel began, but even Stanley could see he had nowhere to go. The Captain cut him off, not unkindly, with a short bark, and Stanley was surprised to see a tear in Abel's eye. There was an embarrassed moment, which was broken by Clamdigger's voice cutting in.

'Captain Anstruther! Erm, the other Captain Anstruther is nearly aboard,' he yelled.

'Great Columns of Fire!' said the Captain. 'That's the quickest work with a boatswain's chair I've ever known,' and he marched off to see. As he followed, Stanley caught Abel's eye, which was no longer moist. In fact, Abel was glaring at him, and Stanley was surprised to see him put a finger to his lips, as if to say 'shhh'. Stanley was wondering what this might mean, when Able Skyman Abel snapped to attention, and Stanley heard a hearty voice from just below deck level.

'Bend, my young sapling, and lend a hand to a better man! I've not climbed four hundred feet up one of your cheap little ropes to be left dangling at the scuppers like a gaffed catfish! And now heave! By my grandma's beard, there's more muscle on you than it seems. Now, where's my big brother on his day of days?'

With this torrent of good-natured banter, Zebediah Anstruther climbed, indeed almost leapt, aboard the Great Galloon. Stanley, now only a few feet away at the Captain's side, gawped at the new arrival. He was clearly a few years younger than the Captain, with fewer laughter lines, and perhaps a slightly slimmer tum, but there the differences stopped. From ponytail to boots, this man was dressed and styled the same as the Captain.

21

'Plum puddings!' gasped the Captain. 'This is embarrassing. My first meeting with my brother in who knows how long, and we've got the same clobber on.'

The small group around them laughed as the Captain took Zebediah in a hug. As they stepped apart, Stanley saw Zebediah set his face in a smile.

'All I need is a hat like an undertaker's chamberpot, and the look will be complete,' he said, and with that he reached out, grabbed the Captain's prized hat, and had it clamped on his own head before anyone could stop him. This caused a collective pause, before the Captain clapped his hands together and smiled.

'It's good to see you, Zeb. You've brought the rings, I'm sure?' he said.

'All the way from the Old Market in Suuk,' said Zebediah. 'And the speech is writ, I'm afraid, Meredith. But where's this bride of yours?'

Before the Captain could answer, Abel's voice interrupted them, calling up from the main ladder.

'Captains, Lady Isabella Croucher is making her way on deck!'

'Ah!' said the Captain. 'She's come to say hello to you, Zeb, I expect.'

But Zebediah's face dropped as he looked at the Captain, then towards the hatchway that the announcement had come from.

'Surely you're not going to let her see you?' he hissed.

'Why ever not?' said the Captain. 'She's seen me before.'

'But not on your wedding day, Meredith,' cried Zebediah, increasingly agitated. ''Tis extreme bad luck. You'll curse your marriage before it starts.'

The Captain tutted and looked around, but there was now no one about to help him. Just he, Zeb and Stanley now stood on deck – everyone else had seemingly gone below to prepare for the ceremony.

'What say you, Stanley?' said the Captain, and Stanley was once again astonished to be included in the great man's conversation.

'Ermm, I have heard it's not the done thing, Captain,' he said. 'But what can we do?'

'Hide, you fools! Hide!' snapped Zebediah.

He said it with such conviction that Stanley and the Captain both spun round, looking for somewhere to hide. Right behind the chairs was a large trunk, which was usually used for storing the boatswain's chair apparatus. Stanley lifted the lid, and saw it was big enough for both of them to squeeze into.

'Captain,' he said anxiously, and clambered into it, as he heard Zebediah hurrying the Captain along.

'Get in, brother, before she's alongside!'

And soon the Captain and Stanley were both inside the musty trunk, hunkered down but not too squashed, as the trunk was a roomy one. The Captain was breathing carefully, and there was just enough light for Stanley to see a gleam in his eye.

'Here's fun, eh, boy?' he said with a smile.

'Wait a minute,' whispered Stanley. 'Why am I hiding?' and together they stifled a chuckle.

Outside, Stanley could hear Zebediah's muffled voice greeting the Lady Isabella. They must have missed her by moments.

Later on, the Captain would ask Stanley exactly what he had heard as they hid in the trunk together, and Stanley would go over it and over it in his head. Although it was indistinct at the time, it was a conversation that would change the lives of everybody onboard the Great Galloon, and not for the better. This is what he heard:

Isabella: *Ah! A fine hat for a fine day, my Captain.*

Zebediah: *Why, thank you, madam. And may I say, that is a fine dress for a fine woman.*

Isabella: *Thank you, thank you, my dear. No need to kneel, I assure you. Now, where's that brother of yours?*

Zebediah: *Not here, thank goodness.*

Isabella: *Oh? Is something the matter?*

Zebediah: *I fear so. My brother seems to be planning something. We must act quickly.*

| Isabella: | But, Captain, whatever can you mean? |
| Zebediah: | I'll speak plainly. He means to dupe you, and marry you himself. He has arrived here today looking so similar to me that only someone who truly loves me could tell us apart. |

Inside the trunk, Stanley saw the Captain's shocked expression. Was this some wedding-day jape? Had they misheard? Before Stanley could react, he heard steps approaching, and Able Skyman Abel's higher voice cut across Zebediah's.

Abel:	(Entering stage left) Captain, I'm terribly sorry to interrupt, but the ceremony awaits down below. We must hurry. Where is Captain Anstruther?
Zebediah:	I am Captain Anstruther, curse you!
Abel:	Of course, I mean our Captain, your brother.
Zebediah:	See, Isabella, his cohorts begin the deception already. We have no time. We must find a way, any way, to get away from here.
Isabella:	Leave the Galloon? But . . .
Zebediah:	We shall return, and reclaim it – but no one here can be trusted. Even Abel here

	is playing his part. It is you and me against the world, my darling!
Abel:	*Sir, what is this? Lady Isabella – you do know that this is Captain . . .*
Zebediah:	*Of course she knows me, you two-faced lubber! We are to be married today, and nothing you can say will deter us, if we must run to the ends of the earth to do it.*

At this, inside the trunk, the Captain seemed to be jolted into action. With eyes burning, he leapt up from his hiding place, sending the lid crashing back. Stanley jumped up beside him, but wasn't quite tall enough to see out. As he scrambled over the edge of the trunk, he heard the Captain beside him roaring.

'Zebediah! If you think my wife-to-be will believe your lies, you have another . . .'

But before this sentence was complete, Stanley heard Isabella's voice again, and looking up from where he had flopped onto the deck, he was astonished to see her jump into the arms of Zebediah, who was still wearing the Captain's hat.

'He's here, Meredith!' she said, apparently to Zebediah. 'I'm with you, my love, to the ends of the earth! Where can we go? Where will we be safe?'

While the Captain stood agog, fists clenched, Zebediah lifted Isabella from the deck, and cast about

him like a hunted animal. Beside him, Abel drew his rusty sword.

'Unhand the lady, you scoundrel!' he said, and Stanley was surprised to see rage in his eyes. But Zebediah merely turned and ran towards the taffrail, where he had leapt aboard just a few minutes earlier.

'The boatswain's chair!' he cried, and he deftly flung Isabella into the little canvas seat. He turned, just as the Captain seemed finally to understand what was happening.

'Well, brother,' said Zebediah. 'It seems you have turned my crew against me, and you have charge of my beloved Galloon. But I have my bride, and my integrity. Two things you can never take from me!'

At the commotion, a few people were coming up from below – Stanley saw Mr and Mrs Wouldbegood, and Cook in his best whites, amongst a few others. They looked confusedly from one Captain to the other. Abel made a move towards Zebediah, who quickly flipped Isabella, in the boatswain's chair, over the side of the Galloon. There was a gasp from the people, and the Captain clenched his fists.

'Zebediah,' called the Captain. 'Please! We can talk!'

'Hah!' came the reply. 'Still you persist! Back, all of you! This mutiny will not go unpunished! I will return!'

'But, Captain!' called Cook, and Stanley was

28

surprised to see he was talking to Zebediah. 'We are with you!'

'Too little too late, Chef,' said Zebediah, as he wrapped the rope of the boatswain's chair around his forearm. 'But know this – any of you who resist this man until my return will be rewarded. And Zebediah – two can play at the hijacking game. Your Grand Sumbaroon will serve until I can raise the force to retake my Galloon. Treat her well, you fiend!'

And with this dramatic call, and a flamboyant gesture of defiance, Zebediah leapt overboard, sending himself and Isabella flying towards the sea. In the boatswain's chair, Isabella let out a scream. All the people on the deck, a sizeable crowd now, rushed to the rails to look. Stanley saw the chair plummeting, with Zebediah hanging from the rope, and Isabella's hair streaming in the wind.

Directly below, the Sumbaroon was floating like an alligator, with a hatch open, waiting for them. Behind him, Abel and the Captain were trying to halt their descent by stopping the pulley from spinning, but it was too late. Stanley watched Zebediah's distant figure land on the hull of his Sumbaroon, and take Isabella in his arms again. They swept together into the hatchway, and Stanley thought he just saw Zebediah give a tiny mocking salute skywards, before the hatch was slammed shut. The water began to churn again as the Sumbaroon began to dive. Stanley, still stunned, turned to see what was happening on deck.

Skyman Abel was standing by the pulley, with the rope in his hands, looking utterly shocked. The Captain, beside him, began to shout, 'Weigh anchors! Man the mizzen'bloons! Haul up! We must give chase!'

The small crowd around them shuffled awkwardly, most of its members looking at their shoes.

'Come on,' said Stanley. 'You heard him!'

'Shush, boy!' said a gruff man in the crowd. 'This is not your Captain.'

'He's Zebediah,' cried a woman, from the growing hubbub. 'And I for one shall take no orders from him!'

'Aye!' said another voice. 'We wait here, as long as it takes for the Captain to return and reclaim his Galloon!'

Stanley could not believe what he was hearing – surely people could recognise their own Captain? But then, he had been with the Captain all along. Perhaps the likeness between the brothers was even better than he thought.

He was about to pipe up again, when Skyman Abel's voice rang out. 'This *is* your Captain, you fools! Someone steals his hat and you instantly forget him? I say, what kind of a crew are you?'

'Well . . .' said the man who had spoken first. 'The other man looked like the Captain to me.'

'Of course he did,' said Skyman Abel, incredulous. 'They're brothers. They were wearing the same clothes. But can you not see our Captain's noble bearing? The dignity in those shoulders? We must make chase: Lady Isabella is not safe!'

'We should wait here, I reckon,' said the woman. 'Put this here Zebediah in chains, and wait for the Captain to come back. All in favour?'

Before anyone could say anything else, Captain Anstruther took two mighty strides, and leapt on top of the trunk in which he had been hiding with Stanley. His eyes were pink and tears ran down his cheeks, but Stanley shivered at the fierce look on his face. The growing crowd fell silent. The Captain spoke, quietly it seemed, but his voice carried effortlessly over the whistle of wind in the rigging.

'People of the Great Galloon. I am Captain Meredith Anstruther. I built this vessel with my own two hands. I know each of you by name, and would trust each of you with my life. I ask no one to come with me, but by the lights of the night sky I shall follow this thieving brother of mine across water, earth and fire. I shall take back my beloved, whom he has deceived, and I shall marry her here on my home, the Great Galloon. This I shall do with no rest or play until it is accomplished. Stand with me forever or leave at the next port. But do not get in my way.'

31

The crowd shifted again. They seemed convinced now, but no one wanted to pipe up first. Then Stanley saw young Clamdigger at the back. He took off his blue bandana, and waved it in the air.

'Three cheers for Captain Anstruther!' he yelled. 'Hip hip . . .'

'Hooray!' called a large portion of the crowd.

'Hip hip . . .'

'Hooray!' called everybody present.

'Hip hip . . .'

'HOORAY!' they yelled at the top of their lungs, and meant it.

'Now let's get moving!' called the Captain, and around Stanley, the crew of the greatest vessel the world had ever seen leapt to their well-practised positions. The chase was on.

A few weeks later, the Galloon was heaving through the low grey clouds of early winter, and onboard, almost everybody slept. There were a few people prowling around, pulling on ropes, winding capstans and generally keeping her on track. And there was Stanley and his best friend Rasmussen sitting wrapped in blankets, looking down at the clouds.

They weren't often up at this hour. Stanley was a legendary sleeper, and had once slept quite through the end of the world, only to wake up once it had all been set right again – but something had made them both feel that now was a good time to be awake. They could feel adventure in the air.

Stanley scratched his horn – a small one, like a tiny unicorn's, but crumpled and blunt – and Rasmussen hummed a waiting song. They had been sitting for a while, waiting for the adventure, but had seen no sign of it since the Captain's wedding day.

'It might take months, or even years, for the Captain to catch up with his bride,' Rasmussen murmured.

'Then we'll just have to keep our eyes open for other adventures along the way, won't we?' said Stanley.

Birds flew alongside, but none of them looked like an enchanted princess trying to attract their attention. The mountains loomed way off in the distance, but they didn't look like they were going to turn into giants, bent on revenge. The team of Gallooniers in the middle distance weren't in the process of becoming soulless zombies, hell-bent on mutiny. All was calm. But Stanley and Rasmussen were happy to wait. They knew from experience that once adventure came, they wouldn't get a chance to sit and hum. Adventure had come to them often over the course of their short acquaintance, but they hadn't yet known an adventure that they, and the Great Galloon, couldn't get the better of.

Some people say that the Great Galloon of Captain Meredith Anstruther is the largest ship ever built anywhere in the whole world at any time, including the Queen Beetrix, the SS Great Goodness and the HMS Frighteningly Huge. Others say 'pish' to this, by which they mean 'pshaw' or 'that's simply nonsense'. For these people believe that the Great Galloon isn't a ship at all, but a hot air balloon of incredible size. You shall have to decide, as you read these adventures, which side you agree with, if either.

'The sun is getting warm,' Rasmussen said, shaking Stanley from his thoughts. 'The ice on the rigging is melting away, and I can see Cook is stoking up the stove. It's time for a hot cup of tea.' She jumped up from where she'd been sitting on a greasy coil of rope and hopscotched towards the hatchway that led to the lower decks. Stanley, being slightly less of a morning person, stood up slowly, wrapped his blanket more tightly around his furry shoulders, and trudged off after her.

As he caught up, however, he felt an immense rumbling noise grumble through his whole body. It started in his toes and made his knees shake and his bottom wobble.

34

Next to him the same thing was happening to Rasmussen – he watched her ponytail jump like an eel. This was before he even started to hear it. When the sound hit his ears, it was like nothing he'd ever heard before, and twice as deep. It lasted for thirteen seconds, and he had time to watch the rigging shake and the hatchways jump as the sound boomed and growled around the ship. Looking up, he saw that even the Great Galloon's big balloon was shivering like the biggest jelly ever made.

'Th-th-that's f-f-un-unny,' he said to Rasmussen. 'I don't remember reading on the notice b-board about a te-terrifyingly loud rrrrrumbling noise being pla-a-anned for this moooorning. Perhaps I missed it, or perhaps we're being attack-ack-acked again. Either w-way, I hope it doesn't interfere with our ad-ad-adventure.'

After thirteen seconds, the noise stopped as abruptly as it had started. Stanley noticed Rasmussen waiting to see if it would happen again. It didn't, and nothing else terrifying or unusual seemed to follow it, so they wiggled their fingers in their ears, and went on their way. A cup of tea was even more in order now that there was a mystery to hand.

Captain Meredith Anstruther had heard the noise as well. Usually he would have no truck with these things – he had other things to think about – but this noise worried him. Since his disastrous wedding day, he had spent most of his time prowling the decks and corridors of the Great Galloon day and night, checking the tension of the huge guy ropes, changing candles before they had a chance to die, and shouting, 'Twelve o'clock, and all's well,' in his rolling, chestnut voice.

Of course he didn't always shout that. If all wasn't well – or it wasn't twelve o'clock – he would shout, 'Six o'clock, and there's bears in the wheelhouse,' or, 'Three o'clock, and my bunions are throbbing,' or whatever seemed appropriate. More often than not, all was indeed well, but not now.

He had been high up in the rigging when the sound first hit and had felt the thrum of the wind on the ropes. He had clung on and waited it out, holding his second-best tricorn hat on his head and gritting his teeth, then stormed back to his office, from where he felt able to cope with any emergency. He reached out for the speaking tube that stuck out from the cabin wall and used it to announce, 'All senior crew members report to the Captain's cabin at once. An enormous noise has been heard onboard, and I'm too busy to be distracted by such things for long. We must get to the bottom of this right away!'

Stanley and Rasmussen had made it to the mess where people were starting to gather, and there was a general hubbub of concern about the place. They pushed their way, politely but firmly, to the front of the queue (Stanley used his horn, but only a little bit), and soon they were the proud owners of two big bacon and banana sandwiches and two steaming hot mugs of tea. This mission accomplished, and with ketchup dripping on their shoes, they approached Clamdigger.

'Do you know what's going on?' Stanley asked him, once they had squeezed themselves into a quietish corner of the ever busier galley.

'No,' he replied. 'I'd love to be a fly on the wall in the Captain's cabin, though.'

'Me too,' said Rasmussen. Stanley knew she was thinking how much fun it would be to be able to walk up walls and never have to go to lessons.

'Of course, it'll no doubt be me who'll have to do the actual work, once they've thought of a plan. I wish we could hear what's going on in there.'

'Me too,' said Stanley, who was thinking how great it would be to be able to hear things from four floors away. 'But the only way we could possibly do that would be to go and ask if we can join in the meeting.'

'Yes,' said Rasmussen, 'or to squeeze into the forgotten storage space above the Captain's cabin, and open the tiny secret hatch that will allow us to see and hear every word without the possibility of being seen ourselves.'

'Oh,' said Stanley. 'Is there one of those?'

'Yes,' said Rasmussen, licking ketchup off her thumb. 'But we can't go in there.'

37

'Why not?' said Clamdigger, on tenterhooks.

'Because we haven't finished our tea,' she said. She took a big slurp, and sat back, satisfied.

A few minutes later, with sandwiches scoffed and tea drunk, Stanley and Rasmussen hurried down to the Captain's cabin. Clamdigger had things to do and wouldn't fit in the secret space anyway, but they had promised to report back all that they heard. They got to the door of the cabin and could hear the mumbles and grumbles of a group of grown-ups talking in serious tones. Rasmussen braced herself, legs against one wall of the corridor, back against the other, and began to ease her way up the wooden walls.

Stanley watched her admiringly until she was at head height, and was just about to climb up himself, when a huffing and puffing noise told him that someone was coming. He leaned nonchalantly against the wall and began to whistle – always a sure sign of innocence – and not a moment too soon.

The tall, thin figure of Skyman Abel came panting down the corridor and almost tripped over Stanley where he stood. He stopped when he noticed Stanley and stood directly under Rasmussen, who was still braced against the wall, just over his head.

'Crumplehorn!' he cried and ruffled Stanley's hair. Stanley didn't like being addressed in this way, especially by someone who then ruffled his hair. 'Up to no good, I assume? Like always, eh?'

At this Stanley chuckled, but not at what Abel had said. Rasmussen, now sitting on a beam inches from Skyman Abel's head, was using her ponytail to imitate a moustache and pulling a wide-eyed, big-toothed face that captured his pomposity exactly. But Abel thought Stanley was laughing at his jokes.

'I bet you are, you little tike! I remember when we, erm . . . Well, when you and I . . .' Of course, Abel couldn't remember anything that he and Stanley had done together, except when he had hidden under the seat cushions on the day of the Captain's wedding. He didn't want to bring this up, so he finished his sentence with a nervous cough and a wiggle of his moustache.

'Where's your little friend, Rogerson? Er . . . Rambutan. Rapscallion! Shaken her off, have you? Hah! You pair of tikes!' He went to ruffle Stanley's hair again, but this time Stanley bared his sharp little teeth and Abel stopped halfway.

By now Rasmussen was pulling such a grotesque face that she was in danger of falling backwards off the beam, so it was a good job that Able Skyman Abel said, 'Well, I can't stand here chatting all day. I've been called to a very important meeting. You won't have noticed, but something untoward has been going on, and I've no doubt it will be up to me to sort it out!'

At this, he puffed himself up preposterously, and Rasmussen did the same, making her look like a little mother hen on the beam. Stanley laughed again.

'Yes, I knew that would make you happy. You can rest easy, now that Able Skyman Abel is on the case! You fluffy little scamp!' And, unthinkingly, he ruffled Stanley's hair one more time and yanked the door to the Captain's cabin open.

Stanley was reeling slightly from being called 'fluffy' – although he was covered all over in fine grey-blue fur, he tended to think of himself as normal and everyone else as unusually bald – but he just had time to catch a glimpse of a roaring fire and the Captain standing behind his desk, leaning on it with both fists.

'Friends. Thank you for coming. I believe the Galloon is in danger. Grave danger. Abel, close the door.'

And Abel did.

GOODNIGHT!

At around the time the first noise was heard, Cloudier Peele had been trying very hard to feel sorry for herself. She was hundreds of yards above the Galloon, and

about half a mile behind it, sitting in the spartan but comfortable basket of a small hot air balloon, which served the Galloon as a weather station. She was tethered by a long thin rope to an iron ring set in the deck of the Galloon and was, in theory, watching out for the Sumbaroon, bad weather, and land.

She had a supply of little rocket-shaped capsules that clipped onto the rope, in which she could place a hand-written note. She would then wind up the clockwork key on the side of the capsule and it would whizz away, down the rope, and land on the deck with a loud crack. In this way the crew of the Galloon could get advance warning of any particularly bad weather coming its way.

It was a very responsible job, and Cloudier was secretly thrilled that she was entrusted with it. But the real reason that she always volunteered for weather duty was so that she could spend some time on her own, being pale and interesting. In the basket with her were some cushions and a small side table, on which sat a lamp, some tea and biscuits, and a book of romantic poetry. The book was Cloudier's favourite book ever. It was extremely well thumbed, and had her name written inside the front cover. One day she even planned to read it.

Cloudier wore a long velvet dress made up of black and purple patches. She wasn't allowed to wear make-up, but she had smudged some coal dust on her eyelids and coloured her nails in with black ink. She sat with her legs crossed on the wickerwork floor of the small balloon, and thought about how unfair her life was.

Unfortunately for Cloudier's gothic sensibilities, her life couldn't have been happier. She had a loving family, lots of friends, and was doing well at school. She was fair to excellent at most sports she turned her hand to, and had an aptitude for music and public speaking. She was furious about all of this, and couldn't understand why people didn't resent her, or bully her, or make her feel small, so she could write long poems about her inner turmoil. As it was, whenever she tried to write a poem about being misunderstood, it won a prize and she got her photo in the paper. She couldn't even bring herself not to smile in the photo, because she knew it would embarrass her mother. And so, in her own way, she had something to feel hard done by about.

She was partway through writing a poem called 'O Clamdigger, the Cabin Boy on the Ship of My Soul', and it was this that she was working on as she sat in the balloon. She and Clamdigger were just very good friends, but she thought an unrequited love was a necessary part of being a poet, so he happily went along with it. She was just getting started on verse 129, and trying to find a rhyme for 'invisible' (was 'whizzable' a word?), when the incredible noise struck.

Even from her vantage point, Cloudier could hear it, and she soon felt it coming up the lifeline rope. When it arrived it shook the weather balloon so hard that her teapot fell off the table. She picked it up and peeked over the side of the basket. Although she was so far away, the Galloon still looked reassuringly enormous as it ploughed its way through the clouds. From here the noise sounded like a million angry wasps caught in a huge metal bottle, and Cloudier could not for the life of her think what it could be.

She could see the Galloon shivering slightly, as if it were going out of focus, and she reached out to touch the rope. It was buzzing like a chainsaw, but Clamdigger himself had tied the knots that connected the rope to the basket, so she knew she could trust them. The noise on the Galloon began to fade away, and Cloudier was just settling down again when she heard something else.

The rope was thrumming now in a more familiar way – someone was sending her a message! She clapped her hands delightedly, and then remembered to be a bit less excitable. She shrugged and sat down again with her back to the rope, as if she didn't care. It took about thirty seconds for one of the capsules to make its way up the rope, and the noise it made got higher pitched as it grew closer. As it finally arrived and smacked into a metal plate at the top of the rope, a small firework in its nose went 'crack' to announce its arrival. Cloudier left it a minute or two, to show the universe that she wasn't at all bothered by such fripperies as mail. When she couldn't stand it any more she jumped up, spun round and ripped open the note that was now protruding from the capsule on a jointed arm. She read:

Dear Ms Peele,
   There has been a disturbance onboard the Galloon. All is well, but the source of the disturbance is unknown, and the Captain has called all senior Gallooniers to his cabin. Personally, I fear the worst – keep an eye out for BeheMoths.
   Yours, Ms Huntley (navigator)

P.S. Depending how long the meeting is, I may not be back in time for tea. There's a casserole in the oven. Maybe later you can read me some of your wonderful poetry. So proud, darling. Love, Ms Huntley (your mum).

Cloudier sighed and rolled her eyes. Then she put down the letter and picked up a large pair of brass-bound binoculars, so heavy she had to use both hands. She raised them to her eyes and scanned the horizon behind her. There, just visible at the edge of sight, were some tiny winged shapes, no bigger at this distance than a mosquito, but moving quickly.

Hmm, thought Cloudier. *Probably just Seagles, but I'd better keep an eye on them. You can never be too careful.*

Stanley watched as Rasmussen pulled back a loose board in the wall above the door of the Captain's cabin, and a few moments later they had both climbed up and squeezed into the fusty, cobwebby storage space. Rasmussen slid aside a hatch the size of a postcard, and they each put an eye to the hole.

The Captain's cabin was a snug, warm room with lots of dark wooden tables and chairs covered in interesting instruments of all shapes and sizes. Above the fireplace was a large painting of the Galloon in full sail, at which the Captain was staring inscrutably. Able Skyman Abel had sat down on a bench by the door. There was a number of people in the room, some taking notes, some scratching their heads in a thoughtful way, others pacing up and down. The Captain was still standing behind his desk, and when he spoke again everyone stopped and listened. Even in the space above, Stanley and Rasmussen held their breath.

'What do you think?' boomed the Captain. 'Is she finally breaking up? Are we doomed, do you think?'

46

Captain Anstruther didn't mince his words, which was often a good thing, but sometimes put the wind up people. Not Rasmussen though, who often laughed out loud at his most doom-laden pronouncements.

'Er, no sir, I hope not,' said Able Skyman Abel. 'I think the old Galloon will last a little while yet. At least I hope so.'

'I think you're right, Abel. I didn't build this beast to fall apart at the first sign of trouble. So if it isn't the old girl cracking into pieces, then it must be something else!'

'Freak weather, sir?' said a large woman in a tall felt hat.

'No. It's cold alright, and if we were on the sea I would agree that perhaps a huge rumbling and cracking noise could be made by the ice sheet rubbing and grating on the hull.' As he spoke, he poured coffee from a pot at his elbow into a mug the size of a saucepan. 'However, we are not on the sea; we are three miles above it. And ice doesn't float in the air, except briefly, in the form of snow.'

'Or hail, sir,' said a young man with an eager face like a terrier's.

'Good man, Yorkie. Or hail, indeed. But I ask you this – does hail get big enough to rub and grate on the hull of a Great Galloon, causing a huge rumbling and cracking sound?'

'Not in my experience, sir. But that doesn't necessarily mean it never does,' said Yorkie, throwing more coal on the already white-hot fire.

'No, indeed. But we must work on the assumption that it isn't an iceberg in the sky, as I have never heard of such a thing anywhere in the world,' said the Captain. 'Agreed?'

'Agreed,' they said, except for a tiny man in furs who began to say, 'Actually, in the skies above the Ice Kingdoms . . .' but was so muffled by his scarf that no one but Stanley heard him.

'So we're agreed,' said the Captain. 'It's either more pirates or the end of the world again. I, as you know, have other matters to think about and cannot be disturbed by mere trifles like pirates or the end of the world.'

At this, the Captain's eyes glazed over briefly, and in the pause, many people in the room nodded their heads and said, 'Mmmm.' Stanley and Rasmussen did the same.

'Therefore,' continued the Captain, taking off his hat and passing his hand across his brow, 'I would be grateful if I could leave this mystery entirely in your hands, Able Skyman Abel. If the future of the Galloon appears to be at stake, I shall suspend my greater quest, but not before. You are dismissed.'

With this, Captain Anstruther sat down in his huge, dark leather armchair and began to think, a process that normally required several days, two buckets of hot coffee and a map of the world.

The room began to empty, and Stanley saw Able Skyman Abel waiting around near the door, as if he expected the Captain to suddenly leap up, shout 'Eureka!' and run out into the cold.

'I don't know if it's a good idea to leave it up to Abel,' whispered Stanley.

'No,' said Rasmussen, with her eyes still to the hole, 'but the Captain can't do everything. He's got bigger things to think about.'

'Of course,' said Stanley. 'Maybe it's something we should be looking into . . .'

'Maybe,' said Rasmussen thoughtfully. But Stanley knew she was reluctant to get involved in anything that might distract them from the adventure they were both sure was coming.

They looked into the cabin again, just in time to see that Abel was the last man left in the room, apart from the Captain himself.

'Sir?' asked the moustachioed officer.

'What is it?' grunted Captain Anstruther.

'Just wondered, sir.' Abel shifted awkwardly. 'Any news on the . . . on the other thing?'

'No. That will be all. You are dismissed.'

'Yes, sir.' He saluted, turned on his heel and left.

Stanley and Rasmussen watched as the Captain picked up a large brass instrument like a cross between a clock and an accordion, and held it up to the light. Then he wrote down a measurement on a chart marked 'Altitude', and stared at it intensely for a moment.

Stanley took his eye away from the spyhole.

'Well,' said Stanley. 'Well, well, well.'

'Yes,' said Rasmussen.

'Well, well, well. Well, well, well,' said Stanley, a habit of his that irritated Rasmussen no end.

'We'd better get back to the mess,' she said, to shut him up.

'In case they notice we're gone and start a Galloon-wide search?' he said excitedly.

'That, and because it's nearly time for elevenses!' said Rasmussen, and together they kicked out the loose plank, hopped down into the corridor and began to make their way towards the mess.

The mess was, in many ways, the heart of the Great Galloon. Or the stomach, as Stanley preferred to think of it. There was always a comforting smell of soup, or cake, or curry in the air, and Cook, though slightly scary-looking with his wooden leg, glass eye, bristly beard and gravestone-like teeth, was always ready with a hot mug of strong tea to keep the blues away. As

50

they entered, they saw Abel, with a distracted look about him, pick up a hot cup of tea from the hatch, and put nine sugar cubes in it before settling down at a table near the fire.

'He seems worried,' whispered Stanley as they sat back down to continue their game of backgammon.

'Of course he's worried. He hasn't got a clue what to do,' said Rasmussen, as she crowned two of her pieces.

'We need to do something,' said Stanley. He coughed and held up a small gaming piece that looked like a soldier. 'You can't do that!' he called out in a theatrical fashion. 'This piece is higher ranking than yours! He's just had a promotion!'

This last word was almost hollered across the mess, and to Stanley's gratification, it seemed to snap Abel out of his reverie. Rasmussen cottoned on immediately.

'A promotion?' she said, waving her arms around like she imagined an actor would. 'Whatever do you mean?'

'A promotion!' said Stanley. 'Such as may be given to someone for exceptional service, or loyalty, or hard work in difficult circumstances!'

Abel's ears waggled as he twiddled his moustache. A look of fervour came into his eyes, and Stanley could see his lips moving.

'That should do it,' he whispered.

'Snap!' shouted Rasmussen, banging a counter down

on the gaming board so hard that the table tipped over and all their pieces fell to the floor.

'I win!' they yelled simultaneously. But before either of them had the chance to do the traditional victory dance, the whole room started wobbling for the second time that morning.

Abel Skyman Abel stood up and looked around wildly.

'It's happening again!' he squealed.

'Brace yourselves!' shouted Able Skyman Abel. 'Deep rumbling noise at eleven o'clock! Batten down the hatches!'

But of course nobody had time to batten down their teacups, never mind the hatches, before the full force of the unknown noise hit them all again. The tea on the tea stove splashed and gurgled, the chandelier jumped, the fire spluttered in the hearth, and everyone in the mess held their ears and squeezed their eyes shut tight.

Looking around the room, Stanley saw Mr and Mrs Wouldbegood in the corner, trying to keep their false

teeth in and hold their cups at the same time. He saw Able Skyman Abel's impressive moustache go slightly out of focus as the sound wobbled it, and he saw Rasmussen half laughing and half crying as the noise jiggled her off her chair and onto the ground, where she curled up into a ball.

This time the noise lasted even longer than before – Stanley guessed not less than forty-five seconds. Halfway through it became, to his astonishment, even deeper than it had been, so that the chandelier rattled itself into a hundred pieces, the fire went out and he felt as if his brain would pop. When the noise finally died away, there was a shocked silence in the mess for quite a long time.

'More tea, anyone?' said Cook. 'Pot's still hot.'

It was decided by all that more tea was exactly what was needed. Stanley gripped his hot new mug tightly and sat down again near Skyman Abel.

'So,' he said, leaning over. 'What are we going to do about these unusual noises?'

'Well, I don't think we should panic,' said the Skyman, biting his collar distractedly and sitting down at Stanley and Rasmussen's table. 'As yet I have no idea what's causing it.'

'Neither do we,' Rasmussen said, watching the Wouldbegoods pick broken china off the black and white tiles of the floor. 'But whatever it is, I hope it's friendly.'

'It doesn't sound friendly,' said Stanley, with a finger in his ear.

'But neither does it sound unfriendly,' said Rasmussen. 'And we must give it the benefit of the doubt.' She began to reset the pieces of their game.

'How can we give it the benefit of the doubt?' cried Stanley. 'We have no idea what it is. It could be animal, vegetable or mineral.'

Rasmussen was using her dress to polish a pawn, and he wasn't even sure she was listening, so he raised his voice slightly. 'It could be the sound of the Galloon falling to pieces. It could be a BeheMoth eating the rudder. It could be the noise the sun makes when it's angry. Or worse!' he finished, and flopped back down on his seat.

Beside him, Abel let out a tiny whining noise.

'Well,' said Rasmussen, putting the last marble back in its place. 'As you put it so succinctly, I suppose the sooner we find out what's going on, the sooner we can get back to looking for an adventure. What do you think we should we do?'

'Well,' said Stanley, uncertainly. 'Able Skyman Abel's in charge. What do you think, Abel?'

A tiny squeak escaped Abel's lips, and Stanley noticed that he was now biting down on a spoon with a faraway look in his eyes.

'Falling to pieces . . .' he whimpered. 'BeheMoths . . . Angry sun . . .'

'Oh dear,' said Rasmussen.

Up in the weather balloon, it was raining on Cloudier Peele. Often bad weather didn't reach the deck of the Galloon itself, because of the huge array of balloons, sails, canopies and awnings that it was slung beneath, but for Cloudier there was no such protection. She had pulled an oilcloth over her head, under which she was now hunched, writing in her notebook. Every few minutes she popped out and had a good look through the binoculars, concentrating particularly on the area of sky behind her, where she had noticed the flying object a little while before.

The winged thing seemed to still be following the same course, but as yet was a long way away. The huge birds known as Seagles often followed the Galloon for hundreds and hundreds of miles, and were considered a sign of bad luck by those passengers and crew who believed such nonsense. Cloudier just thought they were beautiful, and had once written a sonnet about them. It was called 'Lonely Wanderer, May I Roam Wi' Thee?'

Cloudier knew better than to pepper her poetry with words like 'thee' and 'wi', but sometimes she couldn't help herself. As she watched through the binoculars, occasionally stopping to wipe drizzle from the lenses, she realised that the flying object wasn't flapping its wings, as a BeheMoth would have done. Seagles could sometimes go for days without flapping, but a BeheMoth, with its thin, papery wings, could not glide in the same way. So a Seagle it must be. She sank back down to the floor of the basket, and carried on working on her great epic, 'Why Do Boys Think it's Funny to Make that Parping Noise with Their Armpits?'

The title might need some work, she thought.

Stanley and Rasmussen spent the morning very productively, waiting for another noise to occur. They played another game of backgammon, which Rasmussen won by two laps. Then they made up speeches and read them out to each other, giving each other marks out of ten. This turned out to be a draw at four hundred and seven points each, so they clambered up to the main deck to read their speeches to the gulls on the figurehead, who would surely declare a clear winner.

As they set out, though, they noticed that a lot of people seemed to be heading the same way. Clamdigger seemed to be hustling people along, and there was a hubbub of chatter in the many and various languages of the Galloon. Something was occurring, and they hadn't been informed. Rasmussen went bright red, then began furiously spinning round in circles, singing a furious song about how furious she was. Stanley knew very well to stay out of the way until she had finished. Before too long, with a slightly dizzy look in her eyes, she was stamping along through the crowd, with Stanley doing his best to keep up.

After many minutes of walking (for the Galloon was so enormous that one could spend hours walking around it without ever crossing the same point twice), they noticed that the crowds seemed to be converging at a spot on the deck near the mainmast. The air was still chilly, and they could see the breath of the crowd rising like a little volcano as they approached. They could also hear, as they got closer, that Able Skyman Abel seemed to have conquered his fear to some extent and was speaking to the crowd in his pompous, piping voice about the recent very loud noises.

'And yet fear not, my friends,' Abel was shouting through a trumpet as they pushed their way towards the front of the crowd, 'for the Captain has put me in charge of dealing with the noise, and I have already formulated a faultless plan.'

People nodded and murmured, happy that someone was taking charge. Stanley was now sitting on Rasmussen's shoulders, so he was at the head height of the rest of the crowd, and he could see that Abel was standing on an old seachest, surrounded by a few of the other important figures on the ship – Cook,

Yorkie the engineer, Ms Huntley the navigator and so on.

As Rasmussen and Stanley came squeezing through the throng, Abel seemed to notice them and addressed them directly. 'Aha! Sorry to start without you two, but you're young and not very important, so Cook here has just been guessing what you might say at each point of the discussion.'

'Oh,' said Stanley, dropping gently to the ground.

'I don't think that's—' cried Rasmussen, but she was interrupted by Abel's trumpet, the horn of which he put right by her ear.

'Deck-scrubbing duty – Cook thought you would volunteer, so you're on for the next two weeks, 'til we reach our next stop-off point in the Eisberg Mountains,' said Abel.

'What's that got to do with—' said Rasmussen and Stanley together, but Abel was off again.

'Awfully bad luck. Lookout duty – Cook thought you would volunteer, so you'll be taking it in turns 'til we reach our next stop-off point in the Eisberg Mountains.'

'What about the noises?' they said again, to no avail.

'And before all that, tidying the stores. Cook has been making a complete mess of the supplies in the hold and has kindly volunteered you to go down and tidy it all up.'

'Wait a minute!' shouted Stanley. 'The hold is gigantic! It's as dark as a lake, and as deep as space!'

'Quite. So, well done for volunteering,' said Abel, pleased with himself. 'While you're down there, you can also bring back enough dinner for the whole crew and all the passengers. It's a job for thirty strong men really, so I was surprised that two small children such as you volunteered. But now you have, you can't get out of it.'

'This isn't fair,' shouted Stanley and stamped his foot.

'I won't do it unless we get extra cake,' said Rasmussen.

Able Skyman Abel looked thoughtful, pulled on his moustache and said, 'Extra cake seems fair enough to me. Any volunteers for cooking extra cake?'

'I think Rasmussen and Stanley might volunteer to cook extra cake,' said Cook, scratching his head with a ladle.

'No, we mightn't!' said Rasmussen, jumping in the air. 'We're here now. You don't get to volunteer us for anything.'

'Good point,' said Cook.

'Good point,' said Able Skyman Abel. 'As punishment for volunteering a crew member who doesn't wish to be volunteered, *you* can cook the extra cake. And you yourself must eat no fewer than three slices per day, so no funny business such as coconut, marzipan or bits of orange peel.'

'Can't say fairer than that, Able Skyman. I shall look forward to it.' And with this, Cook sat down on the seachest, took a notebook and pencil from his tall white hat and began to write cake recipes, with his tongue sticking out of the side of his mouth.

Rasmussen and Stanley shook hands to congratulate themselves on having got out of cooking extra cake, before Stanley remembered.

'What about the noises?' he called. 'Has anyone come up with any ideas as to what they might be?'

'Ah, yes,' said Abel. 'I have been thinking long and hard about the noises that have been troubling us this morning and, as I said, have formulated a foolproof plan. Firstly, they may be nothing. Secondly, they may not happen again. Thirdly, nobody knows what they are, and so we must bear in mind the very famous phrase: what we don't know won't hurt us. Therefore, as first officer on this ship, I declare that the noises are HUUURRRGGGH!'

Of course, Able Skyman Abel didn't really say huuu-urrrgggh. Huuuurrrgggh was just an easy way to show you that nobody heard what Able Skyman Abel said after 'the noises are', because the noise happened again. The whole crowd joggled up and down as if it were standing on a snare drum. Cook's ladle clanged against the metal plate in his head, little Borussia Munro bounced down the stairs with a perplexed look on her face, and Mr Wouldbegood clattered around with his walking stick for fifty-two seconds, which is how long the humongous noise lasted this time.

'As I was saying,' Abel continued gamely as the ringing in his ears died away, 'I firmly believe that the unforeseen noises are very probably KRRROOONNK!'

Of course, you will have gathered that Able Skyman Abel was no more likely to have said krrrooonnk than huuuurrrgggh, and so you will already know that the noise had happened yet again, almost straight away.

Stanley watched as the crew of the Great Galloon bounced around the deck, hanging on to anything they could grab. He and Rasmussen were beginning to get used to the noises by now, so they hunkered down close to the ground, closed their eyes and waited for the infernal racket to stop. This time it was longer and louder than ever, and, after almost a minute, it finished with a thud and a piercing, raucous squeak, like an elephant stepping on a parrot.

'The noises are very probably some kind of practical joke,' said Abel in a tremulous voice, once the noise had died down at last. 'I shall get to the bottom of this and the culprit will be brought before the Captain.'

'But that's silly,' said Stanley. 'How can it be a practical joke? Who could make that much noise? And how would they get here? We're flying three miles over the ocean.'

'Never underestimate the resourcefulness of great practical jokers,' said Abel. 'Many of them will stop at nothing to wreak havoc on the innocent.'

'True,' said Rasmussen, thinking of the time she herself had sneaked into the palace of the King of Thorway to put a whoopee cushion under the Queen's throne. 'But what would be the point of making such a loud noise as a joke? I don't think it's likely.'

'Nevertheless, young lady, a practical joke is what I believe it to be. For if not a joke, then what? Something extremely scary, and that doesn't bear thinking about. I have my promotion to think of, and feel much more able to deal with a practical joker than anything genuinely terrifying. Now, you have your chores, so I suggest you go about them without questioning your elders and betters any more.'

With this, he pointed towards two large buckets of soapy water and two brooms that were leaning on a rail nearby.

'You've plenty to be getting on with,' he said, and with a haughty flick of his magnificent moustache, Able Skyman Abel turned smartly on his heel and strode away, leaving Stanley and Rasmussen none the wiser over the mysterious noises, but with a lot more work to do than when they had woken up that morning.

'Another game of backgammon?' said Stanley. 'I'll bat this time.'

'How can we?' said Rasmussen dejectedly. 'We've got enough chores to keep us from backgammon 'til we get to Eisberg, never mind these adventures we're supposed to be having. Even if an adventure did turn up we'd probably be too busy cleaning, cooking, scrubbing or polishing to notice. In fact, we'd better get started on the scrubbing.'

They dipped the stiff brushes in the huge buckets of soapy water and began to move backwards and forwards across the deck. They couldn't do the whole thing, of course. It was an enormous distance from one side of the Galloon to the other, and there were obstacles such as wheelhouses, storerooms, chicken coops, a fairground and two railway tracks. But they could make a start, and so they did. As they scrubbed, they heard an enormous voice, like a cannonshot booming in the night.

'Nor'-nor'-west by twenty and gain a mile in height! Heave to!'

They stopped jousting with their brooms and turned to look up to the bridge where the Captain habitually stood. And there he was, a huge black shape against the clouds, wearing his enormous hat and holding on to the railings in a highly dramatic way. As they watched, he held an enormous brass-bound telescope up to his eye, squinted at the horizon, took a huge breath and bellowed at the top of his considerable lungs.

'Full ahead! Make all sail! Inflate the mizzenb'loon!'

He then rang a great bell that was hanging from a beam near his head, turned and went out of sight. Looking around, Stanley and Rasmussen saw that the Captain's words had caused a flurry of activity.

Clamdigger, the general factotum on the Great Galloon, started organising a team of men and beasts to haul on ropes to inflate various secondary balloons and move them to different positions. Mr and Mrs Wouldbegood swarmed up the rigging towards the crow's nest, from where they could keep a lookout for obstacles such as mountains or other ingenious flying contraptions that they might bump into, and even Skyman Abel could be seen marching to and fro across the bow of the Galloon, giving orders and shouting in a self-important way.

'Wow,' said Stanley. 'I wonder what all this fuss is about?'

'Maybe the Captain has heard something,' said Rasmussen thoughtfully.

'Well, of course he's heard something!' Stanley rolled his eyes. 'That's what we've been talking about all morning.'

'No, not the enormous rumbling noises,' said Rasmussen. 'Perhaps he's heard something about his mission, his quest, his life's singular goal.'

'Oh, that,' said Stanley, who had almost forgotten,

in the excitement of the noises, that they were still seeking the Captain's nefarious brother. 'So is that why we're going to the Eisberg Mountains? Does he think that's where his poor lost bride might be?'

'Maybe. Or maybe we just need supplies. Only Ms Huntley the navigator knows, and she is sworn to secrecy. I don't think they even tell Able Skyman Abel. The Captain just does what he wants, and if anyone wishes to come along, they can, as long as they help out and don't cause trouble.'

Rasmussen had been onboard the Galloon for most of her life, a fact that she never failed to impress upon Stanley whenever she was feeling cross, which was often.

She was the daughter of the Dowager Countess of Hammerstein, and so often had to get scrubbed pink and dressed in frills and taken to dinners and dances, which Stanley was happy to miss.

It was often after these occasions that she told him some tale of a dashing young hussar who had been eaten by wolves on the dancefloor, or of a butler who turned out to be a dragon in disguise, but he was never sure if this was what had really happened or just a way to make a boring evening into an interesting game. And so, whenever she purported to know more than him about goings-on aboard the Galloon, it could have been something she had overheard at a ball or something she was making up from scratch for a game. Either way, it made sense to listen carefully.

'What if people want to get off because of all these scary noises?' said Stanley, who realised that in all his time on the Galloon he'd seen many people arrive, but none leave.

'Anyone can get off any time, but it's quite hard when we're three miles up, and the Captain won't stop unless we need fuel or supplies. Some people might get off at the Eisberg Mountains, and maybe some new people will get on. But enough of this chit-chat,' she finished. 'We'd better get down to the hold and start tidying up, or we'll never get the job done.'

'Yes,' said Stanley, but he wasn't really thinking about tidying the hold. He was looking up at the bridge, and thinking of poor Captain Anstruther and his lost love.

Cloudier's pen scritched and scratched as it raced across the page.

> *Oh, why do boys not care*
> *About having greasy hair?*
> *And why do they all choose*
> *To wear such stinky shoes?*

She stopped writing, and re-read her words. She was aware that perhaps a note of personal bitterness was creeping into her work of late, but thought she had it under control. She was just about to carry on with a few well-chosen words concerning boys who go to dances only to hang around in groups, when she remembered that she was supposed to be on a state of high alert.

She put her notebook down carefully and stood up, dropping the tarpaulin from her shoulders as she did so. She'd been sitting in the same position for quite a while, and so she stretched her arms to loosen them as she peeked over the edge of the basket. First she looked back, towards the horizon, where the flying thing had been. Nothing – the Seagle must have gone fishing, or just dropped beyond the horizon. She turned and leaned on the leading edge of the basket, facing the Galloon, and was surprised to feel a strong rush of wind in her hair.

It was always a bit blustery up in the weather balloon, but this was something else. She felt as if she were standing in the teeth of a storm. As she stood there wondering what was causing this sudden gale, she realised that she could hear the lifeline keening like a violin string. It was even more taut than usual, and it took a little while for Cloudier to notice why. The Galloon was losing height, and dragging the weather balloon down with it. She blinked and rubbed her eyes, because that's what people in romantic novels did in such circumstances, but it didn't change anything. She could see her home, the almighty Galloon, and many many miles beyond it she could see the horizon, with its majestic line of hazy-grey mountains. And the Galloon was definitely sinking.

Trying not to panic, she began to search around for a mail capsule, so that she could send a message to the crew of the Galloon. She found one under the table, and tucked it under her arm as she snatched up her notebook and pen. She turned over the page – even an emergency such as this wasn't worth ruining a good poem for – and scribbled a note.

> *The Galloon is sinking*
> *And I am thinking*
> *That something is going awry.*
>
> *Please tell the Captain*
> *To find out what's happening*
> *Before we all drop from the sky.*

She read it through again, and winced at the rhyming of 'Captain' with 'happening'. But there was no time for finesse – this was an emergency. She rolled up the piece of paper, and was ready to place it in the capsule, when a huge grey and white bird with a fierce red beak

71

landed heavily on the rim of the basket, and plucked it from her hand.

'CAW!' it said, with a look of malice in its beady eye.

GOODNIGHT!

After lunch, more tea and their first slice of Cook's punishment cake (a bizarre ginger and pickled onion sponge), Rasmussen and Stanley stood near the stern of the Great Galloon by the hatch marked 'All The Way Down', each waiting for the other to open it.

'Have you ever been down there before?' asked Stanley, as nonchalantly as he could manage.

'Yeah,' said Rasmussen. 'Clamdigger pushed me down once, for putting a frog in his tea. There is a series of wooden platforms below the hatch, and I only fell as far as the first one, but I didn't like it one bit. There were tendrils.'

'Oh. Tendrils.' Stanley backed off a little, but Rasmussen grabbed his sleeve.

'And a stink,' she said, with what Stanley thought was a little too much relish.

'Well, if all we find is tendrils and a stink, I think

we should be alright. Anyway, Cook must go down there, if he's made the mess we're supposed to clear up.'

'Apparently he doesn't need to go all the way down. He just stands on the top landing and shouts what he wants into the darkness, like "fifty pounds of spuds" or "a sack of flour", and then he pulls on a rope and it comes up out of the darkness.'

'Who puts it on the rope?' said Stanley, all pretence at nonchalance gone.

'Don't know. Cook doesn't know, either. He said that as long as it worked, he didn't care how.'

'Does the Captain know?' said Stanley, scratching his one crumpled horn.

'Probably. But he's—'

'Got more important things to think about than an unknown helpful creature living in his hold.' Stanley finished the sentence for her, and then looked back down at the hatch, solid and ominous, set into the deck. 'So why do we have to go and tidy it up?'

'Apparently, since even before these noises started, whoever used to put things on the rope and send them up to Cook has stopped. And so Cook's taken to bringing his longest fishing line with him into the hold, hooking the first sack or barrel he can and running back out. He's been making dinner with whatever he's got,' said Rasmussen.

'Hence the pickled onion and ginger sponge cake?' said Stanley.

'And bacon and bananas at breakfast,' said Rasmussen.

'No. That was my idea,' said Stanley, smiling. Nonetheless, the thought of more hideous meals sparked something in Stanley. 'Something must be done,' he growled. 'And it's up to us to do it.'

'Yes,' said Rasmussen, doggedly. And with that, she pulled at the latch, heaved on the heavy wooden trapdoor and dropped it with a clunk against the deck.

'Aah!' yelped Stanley. 'Let's not be too hasty about all this. Let's think things through.'

'What's to think?' said Rasmussen, with her feet already on the top rung of a slimy wooden ladder that stretched down into absolute blackness. 'We've got a job to do, and the sooner we do it, the sooner we can get back to looking out for this adventure we're supposed to be having. Anyway, if anything down here had wanted to eat anyone, or even just bite them in half, it would have done so by now. And I don't think the Captain would stand for that sort of person onboard his Great Galloon anyway. So let's go.'

Stanley couldn't fault his friend's logic, but he wasn't quite as sure as she was that they would be safe. After all, the Captain had done nothing about the terrifying noises that had been paralysing the Great Galloon, so why would he care what was living in the deepest hold?

Nevertheless, he readjusted the sword that he carried in his belt, and tentatively followed Rasmussen through the hatchway. Once through, he held his candle high, and it guttered in the breeze.

They were standing on a narrow wooden ladder and, below them, the daylight faded into pitch darkness. Stanley shielded the candle as best he could with his paw, as they carried on climbing down the almost vertical steps. After a few dozen rungs, the gloom began to envelop them. He cleared his throat – the noise sounded tiny and reminded him how huge the hold was – and spoke.

'Ra-Rasmussen?' he said.

'Yes?' said Rasmussen, her voice sounding as if she was a hundred miles away.

'Are you a hundred miles away?'

'I don't think so. I'm here.' Rasmussen's hand came into view in the dim light from the hatchway. Stanley gripped it tight.

'Okay. Shall we carry on down?' he continued.

'I expect we should. Careful, now. The steps are very slippery, and they seem to be held to the wall with string and tape.'

Although it was hard going, the next stretch of the climb wasn't as long as Stanley had feared. After

maybe fifty more steps, they came to the landing Rasmussen had fallen on in the past, a wooden platform slightly wider than the staircase, but much more rickety. Rasmussen crept onto it first, then Stanley tentatively stepped down. It creaked as he put his weight on to it, and he felt that it was held to the wall of the hold by willpower alone. He felt his way to the edge of the platform with his foot and held his candle higher, for what little daylight there was seemed to be swallowed up by the yawning gulf below. He peered into the velvet blackness.

'What can you see?' whispered Rasmussen.

'Nothing,' said Stanley, truthfully. 'Nothing at all. The ladder just stops a few rungs down from here. We can't go any further down.' He secretly felt relieved at this. 'But you were right about one thing. There's definitely a terrible stink.'

Rasmussen breathed in, and Stanley immediately saw her eyes begin to water. The stink at this level was overpowering. It crept into his head not only through his nose, but through his ears and eyes as well. It made his palms sweat and his hair stand on end.

In the village where Stanley grew up, there was a local delicacy called Pongcheesy Stinkfruit, used to make jam, mosquito repellent and fireworks, but even harvest day in the Stinkfruit Orchards was nothing compared to this. It was all he could do not to run back up the staircase and out into the cold, fresh air. But he didn't, and neither did Rasmussen.

'We must be brave,' said Stanley, who had a keen sense of duty, and an even keener sense of not wanting to eat pickled onion flavoured sponge cake ever again.

'Yes. Brave,' said Rasmussen, holding her nose tightly.

'Maybe we should make sure that what Cook said is true,' said Stanley. 'Perhaps if we shout out a kind of food, it will appear on the platform, everything will be back to normal, and we won't have to go down there at all. Not that I mind,' he added.

'Good idea,' said Rasmussen. 'And we could ask for something to help take this stink out of our heads.'

'Excellent plan,' said Stanley, and he stroked his furry chin while he thought of what to ask for. Behind him, Rasmussen coughed and choked as she tried to fight off the stink.

'I don't think I can be down here for long,' she said.

'Me neither. How about some peppermints?' suggested Stanley.

'Good idea,' said Rasmussen and, creeping to the edge of the landing in the near-total darkness, she cupped her hands round her mouth, and shouted, 'PEPPERMINTS,' as loudly as she could.

They waited for a few seconds, listening to the darkness. Nothing.

'Perhaps you didn't sound enough like Cook,' said

Stanley. 'Let me have a go,' and he too leaned over the abyss and shouted, this time in a voice much lower than his normal speaking voice. 'PEPPERMINTS!' he boomed, and again they listened to the inky silence. 'Do you think this is what Cook pulls on to bring the supplies up?' asked Stanley, tugging gently on a frayed but substantial-looking rope.

'Yes. But I don't think anything's happened. We would have heard.'

'You never know,' said Stanley. 'It may be that someone who spends their life in pitch darkness lugging crates and sacks of food around for someone they've never spoken to, with no expectation of getting paid or rewarded, can do so in total silence.'

'Yes. Or perhaps the hold is so deep that any sound gets lost before it reaches this platform,' said Rasmussen. 'But I think it unlikely. Pass the candle to me, and see if that rope is attached to anything.'

Stanley did so, and, while still a tad wary of what might be on the end of it, he gave the rope a slightly heftier tug. He could tell that it was attached to something a long way down in the darkness.

'This must be it!' he said.

Together they hauled on the rope and were pleased to find that, although it was hard work, it felt like they were moving something far below them closer. After ten minutes of huffing and puffing, the end of the rope was level with their platform, and they were disappointed to see by the flickering light of the candle that there was nothing on the end but a large iron hook, on which sat a fat brown rat, blinking at them lazily.

Stanley moaned. 'Whoever it is who helps Cook out is still missing, and we still have to go down to the hold, tidy it up and bring back supper for four thousand and sixty-two people.'

'Including,' Rasmussen said, 'three hundred and seventy vegetarians, twelve who only eat goat, and a bucket of milk for the giant baby.'

'Well, we better get KKKRRROOONNKKK!' said Stanley, although I'm sure almost all of you will have realised that he hadn't said 'KKKRRROOONNKKK' at all. The noise had happened again, and in the enormous cavern of the hold after the quiet of the last few minutes, it seemed louder than ever. Rasmussen and Stanley held on to the landing with all their might as it bucked and shimmied beneath them. The lazy rat bounced around on its hook like a jumping bean, and then fell into the darkness with a squeak.

The hatchway above slammed shut, so the only light in the hold was now provided by Stanley's candle, which he promptly dropped in shock. Rasmussen was trying to clutch onto the landing, while still covering her ears with both hands.

Stanley saw the candlestick juddering across the landing, towards the edge and the nothingness below. He began creeping after it, with one paw over his left ear, and the other clutching the slimy planks of the landing. The candle shuddered along and threw hideous shadows up the wall. Rasmussen cried out as Stanley reached to grab the candle, moving nearer and nearer to the edge.

All this time, the noise continued and made these events look like a very old film, where the characters shake and move too quickly. Stanley reached as far as he dared towards the edge of the landing. Rasmussen had crawled across the planks, too, and now grabbed hold of Stanley's knees.

Just then the incredible noise stopped, and two things happened. Firstly, Stanley managed to grab the candle and hold it aloft in triumph. Rasmussen shouted something, but he couldn't hear what she said, as his ears were ringing like the bells at a royal wedding. Secondly, the rickety landing they were lying on gave a creaking sigh and came away from the wall, forcing Stanley and Rasmussen to cling on to the gaps between the boards with their fingertips. A noise like nails on a blackboard filled the air as gravity took hold. Stanley and Rasmussen were sliding down the now sloping platform, towards the near-bottomless depths. Stanley gulped. Rasmussen gave a nervous chuckle, as she often did in times of stress. And then they fell.

GOODNIGHT!

By now, Cloudier and the Seagle had reached an understanding. She would sit very still on her cushions, and the enormous bird would stand haughtily on the rim of the basket, occasionally saying, 'Caw'. So far it was working well, although Cloudier was aware that at some point she was going to have to retrieve her warning poem from the bird's hooked beak. This was a job she wasn't looking forward to. So, for now, just the sitting.

Very few people got to see a Seagle up close. They were often seen following the Galloon, but they always kept their distance, and were seen as a token of bad luck by the more impressionable Gallooniers. Able Skyman Abel claimed to have kept a pet Seagle once, which wore a wig and answered to the name 'Pete'. Looking at the mighty specimen now perching a couple of feet from her, Cloudier thought this unlikely. It was fully four feet high, so it towered over her as she sat back on the cushions where she had fallen. It eyed her sternly, and then swallowed her poem.

'You're quite right. It wasn't up to scratch,' she muttered. 'But I must let the Captain know what's happening. He trusts me and I owe him everything.'

The bird made a noise like a steam train being scraped down a blackboard.

'Erm. Please may I stand up now, please?' she said in her best so-polite-she-could-convince-herself-she-was-being-ironic voice.

The Seagle lifted its tail and squirted out a long line of white poo. Cloudier couldn't help but notice that the poo was whipped away upwards. Even in her slightly panicked state, she knew that this meant the Galloon was in real danger.

'Erm,' she added, nervously. 'If I were to write another note, would you eat that too?'

The bird shuffled its feet and yawned. Cloudier took that to mean no, it wouldn't eat the note. She reached out very carefully and got a fingertip to her notebook. The bird watched. She managed to pull the book towards her, and slowly opened it at a blank page. The bird made a low gurgling noise and cocked its head.

'There there, birdie,' said Cloudier, feeling utterly foolish.

'Caw!' said the birdie, and quite right too. Cloudier

now took out a spare pen from her pocket. The look in the bird's eye changed from unblinking indifference to a hungry glare. Cloudier stopped. The bird made the low gurgling noise again. Cloudier had the strange feeling that this was a noise of encouragement. She clicked the lid off the pen, and quickly scribbled a new note.

Dear Captain Anstruther,
I have no doubt you have noticed, but I feel bound to inform you that the Great Galloon is losing height. I will keep this note brief and prosaic, because I am being watched by a big ugly Seagle. He smells of fish and seems a bit mad, but I don't believe he will cause me any harm.
Yours,
Cloudier Peele,
The Weather Balloon

As she signed the note, the Seagle hopped around the rim of the basket until it was standing directly behind her, looming over her shoulder. It was still making the gurgling noise, and it began to lean ever closer. Cloudier moved to put the lid on the pen, and the tone of its noise changed to one slightly more threatening. Cloudier took the lid off again, and the tone lightened. The bird was now very close to Cloudier's ear. Out of the corner of her eye she could see the murderous beak reach past her cheek, and gently pluck the pen from her hand. It stood up again to its full height, and let cry another cacophony of screeching and cawing, which made Cloudier wince. She turned around to see it throwing its thick neck back and forth, as if manoeuvring the pen into position to be swallowed.

'No!' blurted Cloudier. 'That's my best—'

But before she could finish, the bird grasped the end of the pen, leaned right over her again, and began to swish and sway its head around over the notebook. What it was doing was writing, and what it was writing was this.

Meredith, my friend, greetings from the Seagles, Masters of the Four Winds.

I have tidings to make even your blood run cold. You are being pursued by those foul beasts the BeheMoths, attracted by your low altitude and, no doubt, some trickery of your brother's. You were ever blind to his faults. They will be upon you in hours unless you bring the Galloon high out of their reach. As for Zebediah, my spies tell me he has changed his course – look to the Chimney Isles, my friend. For they are his destination, and your destiny.

This girl is loyal to you and brave, if a bit rude

when she doesn't think she'll be found out. Sorry
I pooed in her basket.
Yours,
Fishbane the Wanderer

Cloudier read the note, her mind whirling.

'But . . . But . . .' she said lamely, before mastering herself and remembering her manners. 'But . . . Fishbane, sir . . . erm . . . you didn't poo in my basket!'

The bird clicked its tongue, and picked up the message pod from the bottom of the basket. It dropped the metal cylinder in Cloudier's lap, looked straight at her and winked one red eye. Then it turned, squirted fishy white poo all over her nice purple dress, and dropped into nothingness. Cloudier threw herself at the edge of the basket and looked down just in time to see the great creature open its wings and soar away.

'Right,' she said, after a few stunned moments of collecting her thoughts. 'I'd better get this note sent, and then see if there's anything I can do to help.'

Gagging only slightly, she rolled the note up and slipped it into the capsule, before settling down on her cushion again, next to her small selection of interesting books.

Stanley and Rasmussen had been falling for what seemed like a week, but probably wasn't. After a while they stopped shouting, as it didn't appear to be making a great deal of difference, and they couldn't hear each other anyway. Stanley peered at Rasmussen through the gloom, her ponytail streaming out behind her as she fell, and, tucking the unlit candle under his arm, signalled in the secret sign language they had developed for just such an eventuality.

What do you think will happen when we hit the floor of the hold? he said with his hands.

I don't know what we'll get for dinner. Why do you ask now? replied Rasmussen.

No, said Stanley, still signing furiously. *You misunderstand me. Do you think we'll land safely?*

There are twelve of them. But it hardly seems relevant, signed Rasmussen crossly.

Stanley rolled his eyes and decided that, if they ever got the chance, they should practise their secret sign language a little more often.

The advantage of this exchange was that it took both of their minds off what was below them, and moving closer by the second. Stanley saw Rasmussen squeeze her eyes tight shut and decided to do the same.

Despite falling through the air with their eyes closed, they managed to find each other and cling on. Stanley could feel his ears flapping in the wind and could hear Rasmussen doing her best to hum a little tune, as if she were sitting on the beach with her grandmother, rather than plummeting through the air at a thousand miles an hour, or thereabouts.

And then, just when they felt they would either hit the hull of the Galloon and be splattered like custard or smash straight through and continue falling into the ocean below, something completely unexpected happened. They both braced for the impact, but instead of the solid smack of the mahogany hull, they hit something slightly softer, slightly shaggier, and slightly warmer than they expected.

They heard a gruff, rasping voice say, 'OOF!' as they landed, but when Stanley opened his eyes, the darkness was so complete that it made no difference, and he closed them again.

Stanley and Rasmussen clung on tightly to each other and tried to feel what they had landed on. It felt like a warm wardrobe, with arms, covered in carpet, but they knew that couldn't be it. As whatever it was lurched into a loping walk, Rasmussen leaned over to where she thought Stanley's ear must be, and whispered, 'What are we being carried by?'

'It feels like a hairy hillside, or a cross between a bear and a wall. But I know that can't be it. Perhaps I should light the candle again,' said Stanley.

The thing that was carrying them seemed to expand slightly as he said this, and Stanley had the feeling it was breathing in, and therefore must be a creature of some sort.

'NO CANDLE!' it said, in the same huge, rasping voice as it had used to say 'oof'.

'Okay!' said Stanley, so terrified that he had forgotten his manners.

'Sorry. And thank you,' said Rasmussen, who had been brought up in the best circles.

'NO PROBLEM,' said the huge voice, and Stanley had the feeling that being polite was a very good idea.

'I'm Stanley, sir, and this is Rasmussen,' he said. 'We live on the Galloon, and normally we wouldn't come down here, but we were volunteered to tidy up, and to get food for the crew's dinner.'

As he talked, Stanley was aware that the huge creature had carried on striding through the darkness. Now they had reached a door. The creature put them gently down on their feet, and heaved against the door with its shoulder. There was a dim but comforting light coming from the room beyond, and a warmth that was welcome after the freezing clouds outside and the draughty dampness of the hold. The light meant that finally they could see the beast that had carried them here, albeit not too well, as he was standing between them and the light. Stanley had the impression of a huge, shaggy, man-shaped creature. He could just about make out two impressive, curled horns like a ram's on

89

the creature's head and huge muscles moving over each other as the creature extended a hand.

'I'm the Brunt,' he said, slightly more gently than before. 'And this is my home. Come in, Stanley and Rasmussen.'

GOODNIGHT!

Back on the deck, Clamdigger had finally plucked up the courage to tell someone that he had opened a message from Cloudier despite it being addressed to the Captain. He wasn't sure which was more problematic – the fact that he had opened a message intended for the Captain, the news of the Galloon losing height, or the fact that it appeared to have been written by a bird. Unfortunately, the only person he could tell any of this to was Able Skyman Abel.

'Hmmm,' said Abel. 'Well, of course, the Captain will have to be told.'

'Yes, sir,' said Clamdigger, impatiently. 'And very soon.'

'Of course. Now, let me ask you one thing.' Skyman Abel was pacing up and down in front of Clamdigger,

90

trying to look important. 'This "losing height" thing. Is it good news?'

Clamdigger was slightly taken aback.

'Erm. No, sir—' he started, but Abel jumped in officiously.

'Of course it isn't!' Skyman Abel was now staring meaningfully at the horizon, but with just the faintest hint of panic in his voice. 'So it won't . . . help my promotion, then, if I tell the Captain?'

'Well . . .' began Clamdigger, uncertain how to deal with a superior officer of quite such staggering stupidity. 'If the Captain isn't told, we'll all plunge into the sea, and that certainly won't help—'

'Won't help my promotion!' finished Abel, as if the idea had been his all along. 'So listen up! I've decided that it's very important that the Captain hears about this, but it's also very important that it's not me who tells him. Any volunteers?'

Clamdigger looked around and saw, as he suspected, that he was the only person within earshot.

'Er. Me, sir?' he said, resignedly.

'Good boy! And don't let me see you being so reluctant in future. No place on the Galloon for those unwilling to put themselves forward.' Skyman Abel took out a small comb and began combing his moustache unnecessarily.

'And remember,' he added, as Clamdigger moved off.

'If he's pleased, I'll take the credit. If he's upset, you take the blame. Agreed?'

'Yes, sir,' agreed Clamdigger through gritted teeth, and then he ran off to find the Captain while Abel carried on preening himself.

A few minutes later, Clamdigger found the Captain alone in the wheelhouse with his foot on the wheel and a chart spread out before him on the table. He was holding Cloudier's letter up to the light and peering at it intently. Clamdigger had expected him to be outraged, but instead the Captain merely stroked his beard, stared out at the horizon and said, 'Yes. I had the impression something was wrong, and this note confirms my suspicions. The mountains have been at the wrong angle for a while now, but I can't get a feel for the damn ship while these noises are changing all the vibrations. Thank you, Clamdigger. This note could be vital.'

'It was nothing, sir. I thought you ought to know,' said Clamdigger.

'Indeed. Though you may find it hard to believe, there are men aboard the Galloon who would rather let this sort of thing go unreported than risk my wrath.'

At this, the Captain gave Clamdigger an inscrutable look out of the corner of his eye, and seemed for a moment to stroke an imaginary handlebar moustache. 'All we can do for now is lose some ballast and stay ahead of the BeheMoths.'

Clamdigger, for whom this one-on-one conversation with the Captain was a first, struggled to take everything in. 'What are BeheMoths, sir?'

'Normally we fly too high for them. They latch onto the ship and the balloons, and cause all sorts of damage. I lost the first Galloon to them. And I've never yet found a way to shake them off.'

And that appeared to be all he wanted to say on the matter.

Clamdigger looked through the back window of the wheelhouse, to where the Great Galloon's central funnel sat, squat and black against the sky. And for the first time he noticed that where usually there would be clouds of thick black smoke billowing into the atmosphere, there was the merest wisp, like a summer cloud.

Oh dear, thought Clamdigger, his mind whirling. *That can't be good.*

Although the Brunt tended to speak in short sentences and think long before he opened his mouth, Stanley had the feeling that he was enjoying having company, and through a series of questions they had found out quite a lot about him. The Brunt lived in the hold and had done for many years. He didn't mind that almost no one in the main part of the ship knew he was there, because he liked a quiet life, and he had all he needed. The Captain let him eat all he wanted from the stores

94

and sleep in this hot little room, and in return the Brunt did a job that it used to take thirty strong men to do. He used his immense strength to shovel coal into the furnaces, which heated the air that kept the Galloon afloat. Without him, they would all sink slowly to the ground, and be marooned. He also helped Cook by finding the barrels and sacks he wanted, and putting them on the food loading platform. He didn't have to do this, but he had once, many years ago, embarrassed himself by scaring a kitchen boy to tears, and so nowadays he made sure no one had to come into the foodstore. It wasn't that the Brunt was anti-social; it was just that he rarely offered anything more than a straight answer.

'So you live down here all the time?'

'Yes, Stanley.'

'Do you ever get off when we stop?'

'No, Rasmussen.'

'Do you like it down here, the Brunt?'

'Yes, Rasmussen.'

'Do you ever have visitors, the Brunt?'

'No, Stanley.'

And all the time they asked questions, the Brunt never got impatient or annoyed, but he rarely added any details of his own, as most people would. He moved around his little room with surprising delicacy, finding dusty teacups, wiping them with an old cloth, sorting

95

out a little cracked bowl of sugar and pouring some milk from a big metal urn in the corner into a yellow jug. Finally, after enough questions to make most people snappy and tired, he picked up a battered kettle in his outsized hand, turned to them and said, 'Tea?'

They both nodded eagerly. Tea was one of Stanley and Rasmussen's favourite things and watching the Brunt get things ready had made them both thirsty.

'Follow me,' he said. He picked up a greasy little oil lamp and left the room. Stanley and Rasmussen looked at each other, hopped off his low bed and followed him out. Together the three of them walked down a long corridor, in a bubble of light from the lamp.

Before they had a chance to ask another question, the Brunt turned aside and pushed through a heavy oak door with iron studs all over it, and 'Fire Entrance' written across it in brass letters.

'Hot,' said the Brunt, and, from a shelf just inside the door, he handed Stanley and Rasmussen each a heavy leather hood with a thick brass-framed window in the front, like in a diver's helmet. Once he had it on, Stanley felt as if he was looking at the world from inside a film, although he could hear perfectly and the hood was surprisingly light. Rasmussen looked like a strange little mushroom, especially as her helmet came down over her shoulders and pinned her arms to her sides. He laughed as she bounced off the doorframe and finally made it through the door that the Brunt was holding open.

Stanley stepped into the room just behind Rasmussen and immediately realised that the Brunt had been right. This was the hottest room Stanley had ever been in. In it were lots of heavy, oily tools, such as pickaxes, bellows, a great pair of bolt cutters, a hammer the size of a fencepost and half a dozen different shovels and spades, as if the Brunt was a gardener, a blacksmith and a miner all at once. At one end of the room was a chute, below which was an iron hopper, like a skip, full of coal. In the far wall was a metal door, at least eight feet square, of immensely strong construction, with rivets the size of coconut halves, criss-crossed with thick steel bands. The middle of the door was glowing orange from the heat of the fire behind it.

As Stanley and Rasmussen watched through their darkened visors, the Brunt picked up a great wooden stick, charred and notched with use, and used it to lift the latch on the red-hot door.

'Stand back, please, Rasmussen and Stanley,' he said, and they had no doubt that it was a good idea. The Brunt opened the door with the stick, letting out a blast of heat like they had never felt. He hung his small kettle on a hook at the end of the blackened stick, and thrust it into the fire.

Just a few seconds later he withdrew the stick, which

was in flames, and took the kettle, now whistling merrily, off the hook. He put the kettle on the ground, beat the stick with the cloth until the flames went out and used it to close the door again. Then he picked up the kettle, which was still whistling, and led the way out of the room. Stanley looked at Rasmussen in awe. She seemed similarly impressed and gave a happy shrug. Then they followed him back along the corridor to his little bedroom, almost forgetting to take off their protective hoods.

Over tea, they asked more questions.

'So you keep the fire burning, the Brunt?'

'Yes, Rasmussen.'

'Just you?'

'Yes, Stanley.'

'Can I have more sugar please, the Brunt?'

'Yes, Stanley.'

'Do you ever get bored?'

'Yes, Rasmussen.'

And so on. They learned that the Brunt only had to shovel coal for two hours a day, first thing in the morning, to keep the Galloon aloft. They learned that he did indeed get bored on occasion, but he liked to play solitaire and whittle bits of wood and coal into interesting shapes. He was making a chess set, but only had the pawns so far. He kept up a written correspondence with the Captain, and trained rats and other animals that he found in the hold. They were able to do things for him, such as fetch his slippers, read out interesting excerpts from newspapers, and so on. Indeed, as they talked, one particular rat popped out from under the bed, and began sweeping up around the fireplace and generally keeping the place tidy. Stanley was only slightly surprised to see that it was wearing clogs whittled out of clothes pegs.

'Do you like shovelling coal?' he said to the Brunt once more.

'Yes, Stanley.'

'Do you ever want to come outside?'

'No, Rasmussen. Too cold.'

'Don't you like the cold?'

'Don't know. I would die.'

'Does anything get on your nerves?'

But the Brunt didn't answer that last question straight away. It appeared to Stanley that the Brunt was beginning to come out of himself and wanted to answer with more than a yes or a no. He seemed to be struggling with a thought, as if he wanted to say something out loud, but wasn't sure how it would go down.

Finally, he cleared his throat and spoke again. 'The noise,' he said.

'Oh, yes,' said Stanley, suddenly remembering why they had come down here in the first place. 'The noise. It's not . . . it's not you, is it, the Brunt?'

'No, Stanley,' said the Brunt. 'Too loud. I like quiet. The noise makes my head ache. Stops me from . . .'

And then, as if someone had been listening in, the noise happened again. And down here it was even louder than on deck. It thrummed through the Brunt's little room like a tidal wave, smashing the teacups and making Stanley's horn shudder and his head swell. As the cleaning rat scuttled into a corner, the Brunt clenched his mighty fists and pressed them to his temples.

His collection of whittled coal animals fell from the mantelpiece and shattered. He had his mouth open, but Stanley couldn't tell if he was shouting or not, so loud was the noise this time. The noise carried on, and Stanley watched as the Brunt curled himself up into a tight but enormous ball and pulled his thick blanket up to his chin. Stanley was surprised and upset to see a great wet tear plop onto the Brunt's pillow as he screwed his eyes shut tight.

After a minute and two seconds, the noise died, and Rasmussen stood up from where she had been crouching on the floor. The Brunt was sobbing slightly and still had his eyes squeezed shut. They looked at him, and thought about how awful it must be for him, down here on his own, trying to get on with his thankless work, but being driven to bed and distraction by these awful noises.

'Right,' they said together, but quietly so as not to disturb the Brunt further.

'This isn't fair,' whispered Rasmussen. 'We have to find out what's causing these noises, and make them stop. For his sake.'

'And ours!' said Stanley, his ears still ringing.

'The noise is louder here than anywhere,' said Rasmussen. 'So we must be getting nearer to . . . whatever it is.'

'But what is it? And if it's scary enough to make the Brunt cry, what chance have we got of stopping it?' said Stanley, trying to appeal to Rasmussen's sensible side, but knowing she was right really.

'That's neither here nor there,' said Rasmussen, and actually stamped her foot a little. 'Whatever it is, it's causing all sorts of bother and must be made to see sense. Come along, Stanley, we have a job to do.'

And, taking Stanley's hand, she turned for the door. They stopped and turned in the doorway, and Stanley said, 'See you later, the Brunt. We'll do what we can to help.'

But the Brunt just stayed still, curled up on his bed with his eyes screwed up. They closed the door gently behind them.

'It's up to us now,' said Rasmussen.

'Yes. It's up to us,' Stanley agreed. And with a slight gulp, he set off down the dark corridor again, wondering, not for the first time, whether they would get all this out of the way in time for the adventure to start.

GOODNIGHT!

Of course nobody on the Galloon knew that Stanley and Rasmussen had been having tea with the Brunt. In fact, almost nobody knew the Brunt was there. But the fact that they were losing height hadn't gone unnoticed. People were starting to gossip and many theories were being put forward.

Only Cloudier and Clamdigger knew the real danger they were in, and they hadn't had a chance to speak to each other about it yet. Up in the crow's nest, Clamdigger swung his trusty brass telescope away from the weather balloon, to focus on the pursuing beasts, which were just beginning to heave into view. He could see them flapping their huge wings lazily, as they powered after the floating ship.

BeheMoths weren't evil, but they were dangerous. Clamdigger had heard tales of them from seasoned old skysailors, and he had even doubted their

existence, but now here they were. If the Captain couldn't work out how to take the ship higher soon, these destructive beasts would latch onto it, like they latched on to anything even vaguely edible, and begin devouring the oiled canvas of the sails and the great balloon itself. And they were more or less unstoppable. Clamdigger lowered his telescope, and picked up a speaking tube that was clipped to the mast by his ear.

'Erm . . .' he said, uncertainly. 'The BeheMoths are on their way. To stern. Could someone send up a cup of tea, please?'

In the weather balloon, Cloudier was reading frantically. She had a small selection of her favourite books up here – not just poetry, but story books, reference books, diaries and magazines, and any one of them could have contained something important.

So far, nothing had struck her as useful, although she had learned how to get BeheMoth spit out of a linen smock, and what the collective noun was for BeheMoths. It was a 'foreboding'.

There didn't seem to be any stories about brave Gallooniers ridding their vessel of the terrible beasts through the power of poetry. She looked up briefly to rest her eyes, and suddenly a huge leggy shape swooped down on the little balloon that was keeping her aloft. It fluttered its wings panickily, and Cloudier saw its jaws gape as it flew alongside the balloon.

'Oi!' she yelled, but the BeheMoth took no notice.

'Don't!' shouted Cloudier, standing up from her cushion

'Eat!' She reached down to the shelf and grabbed a book at random.

'My!' She threw her arm back way behind her head, with the heavy book in her hand.

'Weather balloon!' and with this slightly unsatisfactory finish, she flung the heavy book into the air. It only had enough force behind it to tap the BeheMoth on its revolting knee, but that was enough to stop it from settling. It dropped straight towards Cloudier, who saw its skull-like features up close for the first time.

'Euw!' she cried, and ducked just as the moth swooped past her and away. Cloudier stood up again to watch it go, but at that moment the book she had flung came back to her. It landed before her with a heavy *crunk*, and the pages flopped open.

Having lived on the Galloon all of her life, Cloudier was only slightly surprised to realise that the chapter it had fallen open at was called 'The BeheMoths, and How We Frightened Them Away'.

'Ah!' she said to herself. 'That'll do nicely.'

And, ignoring the BeheMoths as best she could, she settled down to read once more.

* * *

Down in the hold, Stanley and Rasmussen had made their way back along the corridor in the opposite direction to the Fire Entrance. They had taken one of the Brunt's old oil lamps, feeling sure he wouldn't mind, and had decided to look in every room they passed, hoping for a clue as to what the noises were.

During the last outburst of noise, they had tried their best to figure out what direction it was coming from. Rasmussen said she thought they were heading the right way – towards the pointy end of the Galloon. So they were now standing in front of an old door with rusty hinges, arguing over who should open it.

'It's my turn!' hissed Rasmussen, indignantly.

'But this is the first one, how can it be your turn?' whispered Stanley, grabbing the door handle with both hands.

'Because it's always my turn first. And I'm older than you,' said Rasmussen, putting her hands over his.

'You're not!' cried Stanley, forgetting that they were being quiet and stealthy.

'I am. I was the Queen of the Congo in a former life. That makes me a thousand years old, in a way.'

'Corks,' said Stanley, thinking how Rasmussen was full of surprises, and before he could think of a comeback, she had wrenched open the door. But inside was just a broom cupboard, albeit one that hadn't been used for a number of years, with a family of mice living in the mop bucket. The Brunt had obviously met these mice, as one of them was reading a newspaper. It clicked its tongue irritably at the intrusion.

'Sorry!' said Stanley and Rasmussen together and closed the door quietly.

'There are dozens of doors in this corridor. We'd better split up. You do that side, and I'll do this.' Stanley moved on as he spoke, and Rasmussen followed.

'Okay,' she said. 'If you find anything interesting, give the secret signal.'

'Why?' asked Stanley, his hand on the next door handle. 'There's no one else here.'

'There might be – behind one of these doors,' said Rasmussen theatrically, and wrenched open the door to what turned out to be a small, mouldy bathroom.

Soon they had looked in almost all the rooms down this corridor, including a room with a dark, forgotten theatre, its curtains hanging forlornly before an empty stage, and a long room lined with bunk beds, each with its own washstand and chamber pot. But they had found nothing that looked like it was capable of making a noise such as the one they were investigating.

In fact it contained nothing more foreboding than the thick, clinging cobwebs that coated their hair and faces every few steps. Stanley realised that it must have been a very long time since anyone had been to this particular part of the Galloon.

He caught up with Rasmussen just as she was about to investigate the last door in the corridor. This one was slightly larger than the others, and slightly more ornate. There was a faint pattern carved in the wood, although it was as covered in dust as everything else down here, and so hard to make out.

Rasmussen knocked politely on the door, waited ten seconds and opened it. She held up the lamp as they peered in, but it was merely another storeroom with empty boxes, some old books and a low table with a smoking candle on it.

'Nothing in here.' Rasmussen closed the door, with a disappointed air.

'Maybe this is pointless,' said Stanley. 'Even the Brunt hasn't been along here for years, judging by all these cobwebs. We're wasting our time.'

'There're no more doors on this corridor, but maybe we should look one floor up,' said Rasmussen brightly. 'That noise has got to be coming from somewhere.'

'Yes,' said Stanley. 'Or maybe we should go back on deck. Surely this is a job for the Captain, or Clamdigger, or any one of a hundred people older, cleverer and more responsible than us. What if we find the thing that's making this noise and it's a herd of wild elephants, or an artillery regiment, or another Brunt who isn't so friendly?'

Stanley had been moving back along the passage,

but stopped when he saw that Rasmussen wasn't going to follow him.

'Stanley!' she said crossly, pulling cobwebs from her hair. 'Don't you dare pretend you're too scared. You're no more scared than I am, which is a bit but not much.' She was now struggling to get the sticky cobwebs off her hands, which was making her crosser still. 'If we meet wild elephants, we'll tame them. If we meet an artillery regiment, we'll rout it. If we meet another Brunt, we'll make friends with it, and if that doesn't work we'll catch it in a cage and drop it off in the snow. And you know all that perfectly well. If you're bored or tired, just say so. But don't pretend you're too little or too scared.'

Stanley should have known that Rasmussen would react like this. If there was one thing that made her cross (and actually there were dozens), it was people making excuses for being lazy. And he knew she was right. Somebody had to find the noise and put a stop to it, and it might as well be them. The Captain was preoccupied, the Brunt was ill in bed, and everybody else was somewhere else, so there he had it. He was just about to apologise to Rasmussen when a thought struck him like a clout on the ear.

'A *smoking* candle?' he said.

Seconds later they were back inside the small store-room, examining the stump of a candle that had been blown out some time in the last few minutes.

'I didn't light it,' said Stanley. 'You didn't light it, and the Brunt's ill in bed. So there is somebody else down here after all.'

And our doom seemed upon us. The beasts were ravaging us, eating all our supplies, down to the very bags and tents they were stored in. No book had warned us of this danger, and were it not for a stroke of great fortune, we would never have made it down from the mountainside.

Cloudier looked up from the book, swallowed hard, and blinked. The BeheMoths were flying past in twos and threes now, and she was hunkered deep in the corner of her little basket. Hoping that the author would get straight to the point, she brought her eyes back down to the page.

At that instant, a storm rent the hillside all around. Thunder raged, and drops of rain the size of gold-fish bowls fell all about us. Lying in my tent, with the death's-head of a BeheMoth just inches from me, I watched as it broke off from devouring my home. Its long antennae waved around, as if tasting the air. Thunder crashed across the valley, and the rain picked up pace. Falling now in sheets, it began to batter the creature and me. I raised an arm to

111

protect myself. Thunder crashed again, and when I looked once more, the beast was gone. All its foul brethren went with it, up to the grey clouds and out of our lives forever. Rain saves play.

'Wow!' said Cloudier, forgetting for a moment to be nonchalant.

Was this it? Had she found the answer to the Galloon's problems? She didn't have long to reflect, because at that moment her little balloon shook and rocked so hard she was nearly tipped out. She clung tightly to the edge of the basket, and peeped over. Below her the sky was now thick with the flapping, dusty shapes of BeheMoths, each one as big as a cow.

Her basket was being buffeted and bashed as the falling Galloon dragged it down into the throng. One of the beasts took an experimental bite at the tethering rope as it flew by, and this was enough to sting Cloudier into action. If that rope snapped, or was eaten through, she would be floating free, held aloft only by her small canvas balloon, in a flock of cloth-eating monsters. It wasn't enough to send a message asking Clamdigger to haul her in. She had to take evasive action.

Secretly thrilled, but remembering to tut and roll her eyes for the look of the thing, she picked up a rocket-shaped message capsule, and threw one foot up onto the rim of the basket. Using the bookshelf as a brace, she pushed herself over until she was balanced precariously on the inch-wide strip of plush that covered the basketwork.

Running past her head was the half-mile long hempen cable that connected her weather balloon to the deck of the Galloon. It wasn't fully wound out just now, but nevertheless the tether stretched out hundreds of yards, through the flock of beasts, to the mountainous mass of sails, balloons, rigging and flags that was the Galloon when seen from this angle. The wind whipped through her hair, and her knuckles whitened as she thought about what she had to do.

Tentatively, she reached past her ear with one hand, and grabbed the taut rope. It was about the same thickness as her wrist. Clinging onto it with one hand and balancing on her knees on the basket's edge, she squeezed open the clip on the back of the capsule with her other hand. She clamped it round the rope, and now she was tottering precariously as the capsule slid up and down the cable slightly, exactly as it was designed to do.

What it wasn't designed to do, though, was to carry a person; even a relatively light person like Cloudier. It was designed for letters, perhaps the odd postcard. But the clasp seemed solidly made, the rope was extremely sturdy, and Cloudier had never heard of any messages dropping off and into the sea. Admittedly, she'd never heard of anyone clinging onto one as it whizzed through the air at breakneck speed. Would it take the weight of a thirteen-year-old poet? She would soon know the answer to that, even if only briefly. She managed to brace her feet against the edge of the basket, just as it was bashed again by a passing BeheMoth.

'I don't care about my own safety; I simply have to warn the others!' she said in a melodramatic voice, and immediately felt foolish. To cover her embarrassment, she threw herself forward, over the edge of the basket and into empty space.

As Cloudier picked up speed and felt the gaping emptiness below her, she had time to think *I hope Clamdigger's impressed by this*, and then to reject that thought utterly, before she slammed into the body of a huge BeheMoth that was chomping its way through the tethering rope.

She felt the jolt as the body of the beast hit her square in the midriff, knocking all the breath out of her. Dust flew from its wings, and it flapped desperately as it was carried along by Cloudier's momentum. She kicked out instinctively, and it did the same. Its six legs beat her two, and she put all her effort into holding on as she was pummelled and flapped at.

She hadn't slowed down, and she was now travelling so fast that the beast was having difficulty flying away from her. Like a deer caught in headlights, it was trying to outpace her, lacking the nous to slip off to one side. Cloudier retched as its hideous feelers tickled her face, and then with a great effort she used her legs to tip its huge body off her. The wind immediately caught it, and whipped it upwards like a skydiver opening a parachute.

Cloudier looked over her shoulder, and saw it flap lazily away until it was flying in formation with its many hundreds of companions. Looking forwards again, Cloudier saw that they were now in the lee of the huge mainsail, a great sheet of canvas covering a full acre of sky, and beyond that the mainb'loon itself, looming like a second sun, deep orange-red in colour and hundreds of yards across. Both the mainsail and balloon were dotted with tiny shapes, and Cloudier realised with a gasp that each shape was a BeheMoth, chomping its way through the canvas.

'Nearly there!' thought Cloudier, as smoke began to rise from the rope by her fingers. As the mainsail hove

115

past her, she could see the little figures of the crew on deck, running around in what seemed like utter confusion. She just had time to wonder how on earth she was going to slow down her descent, when another BeheMoth clipped her with its wing as it passed by.

The blow was like a rap on the knuckles, and it was too much for Cloudier's already weary fingers. She had both hands interlocked on the top of the whirring capsule, but the blow made her loosen her grip just a tiny amount, and then gravity and the wind drag on her black-and-purple floaty dress did the rest. She willed herself to hold on, but to no avail, and she felt a lurch as she went from zipping through the air in a fairly controlled way to tumbling crazily, end over end, towards the hardwood planks many feet below.

She just had time to wonder whether her life would flash before her eyes when a big white shape flashed before her eyes. She glimpsed a manic eye and a hooked beak, and then felt something tug at the hem of her dress.

'Fishbane!' she gasped, with what little voice she could muster.

The great white shape of the Seagle eyed her reprovingly as it flapped its mighty wings, trying to steady them both, before dropping Cloudier fairly gently onto the deck.

116

'CAW!' it squawked smugly.

Still Cloudier was too discombobulated to thank it, so she just watched dumbly as it hopped twice, and then leapt into the air.

'Er – thanks!' she called as the great bird gained height, to which the only reply was another long string of white poo.

Down in the hold, Stanley and Rasmussen were searching the little room for anything that would give them an idea of who had been in there and when. Most of the boxes were indeed empty, but some of them held interesting things. One had inside it a couple of sheets of paper. Rasmussen had a bit of a gift for languages, but when she picked up the top page she announced that she couldn't make head or tail of the symbols and lines on it, and then she passed it to Stanley.

'Means nothing to me,' he said. He had found, in the bottom of the biggest box, a small brass object that he didn't understand at all. It was about the size of a sherry glass, and shaped like a tiny bell with no clapper. He held it up to the light of the lamp.

'A tiny goblet?' Rasmussen said.

'No,' Stanley replied. 'There's a hole in it. I've never seen the like.'

'A peashooter? A funnel? A little toilet? An eyeglass? Part of the plumbing?' said Rasmussen.

117

'Could be any of those things. But what's it got to do with the symbols on this paper? Five horizontal lines, covered in what look like little pictures of ants. Very strange.'

Stanley held the paper and the brass object up to the light. But before they could think any more about what these things meant, they heard a rattling noise. Looking around, Stanley saw that it was coming from a door he hadn't noticed before in the opposite wall. He slipped the brass object into his pocket and, using sign language again, told Rasmussen to hide.

'There's no time!' she hissed. 'We have to hide!'

Stanley rolled his eyes and climbed into the biggest box, as Rasmussen crawled under the table. He just had time to pull the lid over his head before the door opened and a little man came in. He was very small, shorter even than Stanley or Rasmussen, although he was much older than either of them.

He was wearing very formal clothes, like a butler or a magician, and he was carrying a thin black stick, almost as long as he was. Stanley immediately wondered if this man was something to do with the noises, although he couldn't see how one so small and pompous-looking could create such a huge fuss. He held his breath as the man pottered around the room, searching in the other empty boxes.

Stanley caught sight of Rasmussen under the table,

and knew that she was holding her breath, too, because her eyes were crossed. He almost laughed because she looked so silly, but the man started muttering to himself and quite threw him off.

'Mumbleumble amateurs . . .' said the little man. 'Mumbleumble forget their heads if they weren't screwed on . . .'

Stanley's mind was suddenly full of people who could unscrew their heads like jam jars, but he snapped back to reality when the man made a much louder noise.

'Aha!' he said, and held up the piece of paper Stanley and Rasmussen had been looking at moments before. 'Here it is. Of course: see Major Seven. I knew it!' and with the piece of paper tucked under his arm, he opened the door again and bustled out.

Stanley had never heard of a Major Seven onboard the Galloon. There was a Corporal Nineteen and a Sergeant Major Eight-and-Three-Quarters, but no Major Seven, unless he lived down here in this forgotten area of the Galloon.

Rasmussen clambered out from under the table and beckoned to him excitedly. 'Come on!' she said, and eased the door open a crack, to check on the whereabouts of the little man. 'He's got to have something to do with all these noises!'

'Right. Yes. Let's go,' said Stanley. 'Before he goes to

see Major Seven. Perhaps he's got some cannons, and that's what the noise is!'

'Or maybe this man's a lion tamer; they wear smart clothes and carry sticks. But let's follow him and sort this thing out once and for all.'

She ducked through the door excitedly. Stanley followed her and was astonished to see the little man open a small hatch in the floor, and descend a spiral staircase, pom-pomming a little tune to himself and muttering, 'More feeling in the third movement, perhaps.'

'There's even more down!' said Rasmussen. 'I thought we were right at the bottom of the Galloon.'

'There's more to this ship than meets the eye,' said Stanley, hurrying towards the staircase.

'It's a hot-air balloon,' corrected Rasmussen, as she held the hatch carefully open, and Stanley began to climb yet further down into darkness.

Cloudier stood rooted to the spot as the full impact of the scene on deck hit her. The deck itself, the rigging, the sails and balloons were all under attack from dozens and dozens of BeheMoths. And Cloudier knew this was just the vanguard of a vast swarm that was still following along behind. As the sails became damaged and the Galloon lost yet more speed, they would draw up and add their massed jaws to the onslaught.

The crew members of the Galloon were doing their valiant best, but this was no everyday case of marauding pirates or bandits. The foe in this instance had no interest in taking over the Galloon, or stealing its treasures. They just wanted to eat it. No amount of dazzling swordplay or tightly choreographed battle plans would win this day.

The BeheMoths were not intelligent enough to be thrown by the crew's united front, and for each creature that was levered off the rigging and thrown overboard, ten more were ready to join the fray. Cloudier snapped back to attention, and searched around for a figure of authority. There was no sign of the Captain, whom Cloudier would probably have been too nervous to speak to anyway, even in extremis. Her mother was probably in the wheel room, trying to navigate them out of trouble, but that was a long way from where Cloudier stood.

About twenty yards away, she saw Mr and Mrs Wouldbegood, the curmudgeonly old mess janitors, waving their sticks at one of the skull-faced monster moths. As she ran towards them, she heard Mr Wouldbegood's familiar chuntering as he told the BeheMoth exactly what he thought of all these modern insect attacks, and how they wouldn't have dared to do it back in the old days. Mrs Wouldbegood was busy blaming the BeheMoth's parents for not

122

teaching it wrong from right, but Cloudier was impressed to see that this constant streak of grumbling didn't stop them from hooking their sticks under the beast, and flipping it onto its back, where it waggled impotently.

'Well done!' said Cloudier sincerely as she approached the old couple.

'We don't need to be patronised, thank you,' said Mr Wouldbegood, barely looking round.

'Although perhaps some of these people nowadays would be good enough to offer us a word of praise every now and then,' added his wife.

'I did say well done,' said Cloudier, instantly frustrated as always. She carried on speaking before they had a chance to grumble any more. 'Have you seen Clamdigger at all? Or Skyman Abel?'

'Clamdigger? That boy's no better than half as good as what he should have been when I was his age,' said the old lady, nonsensically, as she looked around for another moth to harangue.

'And you curtsey when you speak of Skyman Abel,' went on Mr Wouldbegood, as he shuffled off. 'He's more of a man than you'll ever be.'

'Here he is now,' called his wife over her shoulder. 'Let's see if you've got the good manners to say such spiteful things to his face. I shouldn't wonder!'

Cloudier, as exasperated as she always was by an

encounter with the old couple, turned to see Skyman Abel striding across the deck, a look of barely suppressed panic on his face.

'Skyman Abel,' she called, and ran over to him, only for him to duck behind a water barrel.

'Ah!' he said, as he realised he had been seen. 'Young lady. Just checking the . . . water level . . . in this . . . barrel.' He peered over its edge, and started slightly at the daffodils that were growing in it. He peered at one, trying to cover his embarrassment. 'Good, good. Seems perfectly normal. That's one thing we don't have to worry about. Now, how can you help me? I, that is, you?'

With this, Skyman Abel stood up and eyed the skies. Cloudier could tell that he wasn't going to listen to her, but she pressed on anyway.

'Where's the Captain?' she asked desperately. 'Does he realise just how many of these monsters are coming? We'll never survive it!'

'Of course we'll survive it!' said Abel, craning his neck to see where the nearest BeheMoths were. 'The Captain survives everything.'

'But he's got other things to worry about!' yelled Cloudier. 'Look – Fishbane the Seagle told me that the Captain's brother is changing course – that's what he'll be worried about. And there are millions more BeheMoths on their way. You're in charge, Mr Abel! You need to have a plan!'

Abel quailed visibly, then rallied himself.

'I am sorry, young lady, but the emotional ravings of an overblown puffin and an adolescent girl are not enough to make me risk my promotion. Captain Anstruther left me in charge of that business with all the noises, and they seem to have stopped all by themselves. If things were really serious, he would act. It's not as if you even have a suggestion for dealing with these intruders anyway. Is it?'

At this Abel stopped, because the look in Cloudier's eye had changed.

'Is it?' he repeated, uncertainly.

'Yes, it is,' she said calmly. 'I just need to find Clamdigger. And a big bucket.'

Stanley and Rasmussen stood at the top of the spiral stairs and listened. The staircase wasn't all that long and, once their eyes had adjusted, they saw that it led down into a very large room indeed, lit by a semicircle of candles, some distance away.

It had a wooden floor that would once have shone, but was now covered in dust. A chandelier tried hard to glitter, but there was too much dust and not enough light.

'That last run-through was acceptable,' said the little man, and he made a small tapping noise. 'But when we go again, please try to keep up, percussion. We don't want the thunder roll to come in during the summer dance section again, do we? Do we? No. Then wake up. The Count knows and loves this piece and will be humming along. He will know if we butcher it, people, and so we must not. Your very livelihoods depend on it.'

This really meant very little to either Rasmussen or Stanley, both of whom assumed the little man was mad, but I imagine one or two of you will have worked out who he was talking to. Overcome with curiosity, they crept as silently as they could down the stairs, to get a better look at him and find out what he was doing. What they saw amazed them.

The little man was standing with his back to them on a small podium. Arranged in front of him in a wide, candlelit semi-circle were dozens of other people: large and small, young and old, seated and standing. And each person had with them a contraption of some sort.

Some were large, wooden artefacts with strings attached. Some were small, curved boxes with windy handles, or long wooden necks or pedals. They looked to Stanley like a cross between the least effective circus of all time and a travelling museum of curiosities. He almost snorted with glee – surely this had something to do with the noises they had set out to investigate? Rasmussen nudged him and pointed towards the back of the crowd, almost in the shadows.

There sat a hugely fat man with three arms, holding – or rather sitting inside – an immense coiled brass tube that wrapped around and around his body like a gleaming python of mythical proportions. It rose almost up to the ceiling at points, like a shiny rollercoaster, and had more valves, buttons and keys than a plumbers' merchant, a tailor's shop and a locksmiths' convention put together. He sat resplendent, watching as the smartly dressed little man darted forward and placed the piece of paper they had found on a small stand in front of him. He seemed pleased to have it back.

The small man resumed his place on the podium and continued speaking. 'Now we must try the finale again. It's the only thing letting the piece down. And you know why, don't you, Mr Ramalan?'

The fat man looked up at the sound of his name. 'Yes,' he said. 'I'm sorry, Mr Lungren. I'm trying, I really am. It should be okay now I've got the music. But something's not right with the Boomaphone.' He stroked the nearest part of the instrument, almost as if he were calming a frightened pet.

The man they now knew as Mr Lungren seemed more worried than annoyed, and Stanley got the impression that he wasn't a bad man as he spoke again.

'Do your best, Ramalan. The Count won't take your

127

excuses, and he loves the finale especially. From bar 124, up to the end. Plugs in, and here we go.'

As one, the assembled people seemed to scratch their ears. Then Mr Lungren started swinging his baton lightly, in time to a rhythm in his head. On the fifth swing, many of the instruments jumped into action. Handles were turned, strings were plucked and a clamorous sound reached the ears of Stanley and Rasmussen as they watched from the stairs. It wasn't particularly pleasant, but it was music. There was a rhythm there, and Mr Lungren looked very much in control, but the overall effect was of a thousand pianos falling off a cliff.

'I wonder who he means by "the Count", said Stanley into Rasmussen's ear.

'I think he must mean the Count of Eisberg. I hear he loves to listen to music, and we are on our way to his court in the mountains. But we should carry on our search. This is very interesting, but certainly not the noise we're investigating.'

'You're right,' said Stanley. 'And anyway, I don't like it much!' They giggled quietly, and were just about to leave when Stanley remembered the small brass implement he had found.

'This must belong to one of them,' he said to Rasmussen. 'They don't seem dangerous. Let's wait for a suitable pause and hand it to the little smartly dressed man with the keep-in-time stick.' He pointed at the conductor, waving his long black stick around gracefully.

'Mr Lungren,' said Rasmussen. 'Good idea.'

But before the orchestra came to a natural halt, the hideous rumbling noise came again. And it was, again, louder than ever. Both of them dropped to their knees on the stairs and covered their heads. Through watering eyes, Stanley looked up at the orchestra and, to his immense surprise, saw the Boomaphone player, cheeks puffed out like pumpkins, blowing as hard as ever he could, all three arms flailing wildly, pressing valves, twisting knobs and pumping bellows.

The other orchestra members had pained expressions on their faces, but were obviously not suffering in the way that Stanley and Rasmussen were. In fact Rasmussen was now bumping down the stairs on her bottom, while Stanley clung to the banisters for all he was worth. The noise lasted for one minute and four seconds, and when it stopped, their ears carried on ringing for another minute. Stanley looked at Rasmussen and they said together, 'The Boomaphone!'

GOODNIGHT!

Stanley and Rasmussen ran down the rest of the steps and into the full view of the orchestra, who stopped what they were doing and all turned to look, including Mr Lungren, the keep-in-timer.

Nobody was talking. Stanley and Rasmussen started to feel very small as they stood staring at everyone, not sure what to say now the moment had come.

'Ermm . . .' said Stanley.

'Good afternoon, everybody. My name is Marianna Rasmussen, and this is my friend Stanley.'

'Marianna?' said Stanley. 'Is it really?' He'd never thought to wonder whether Rasmussen was a first name or a second name, and he didn't have time to dwell on it now, as she carried on in her best 'being presented to polite society' voice.

'We couldn't help but overhear your beautiful performance, and felt that we had to come in and congratulate you all. We also believe that this may belong to the Boomaphone man.' She held up the brass implement, at which Mr Ramalan's eyes lit up.

'We also wondered if you wouldn't mind awfully not playing the Boomaphone at full volume, as it is upsetting the crew of the Great Galloon, and causing our friend the Brunt to be unable to do his job or have any fun. It is also leading to rumours that there is a dragon or a dinosaur loose on the ship, which can only be a bad thing . . .' She trailed off slightly,

131

as every member of the orchestra looked at her blankly.

'Perhaps they speak another language,' said Stanley. But Mr Lungren was frantically waving his stick in the air, to get the attention of his orchestra. Once they were all looking in his direction, he bent down, and picked up a large piece of black cardboard. Written in white across the top of the card were the words:

The Bilgepump Orchestra

and underneath, in a larger, bolder hand:

Earplugs Out!

As Stanley and Rasmussen read this sign, they heard a faint popping sound, and then another, and then another and many more as the members of the Bilgepump Orchestra unplugged their ears. When they had all finished, Mr Lungren turned to Rasmussen and said, 'I'm sorry, we didn't get a word of that. Could you say it again?'

'Slosh 'im!' came the cry, and another BeheMoth was drenched. It fluttered its wings irritably, but didn't pause in munching on the store yard webbing.

'Keep 'em coming!' yelled Clamdigger, unabashed, as the empty bucket was dropped on the floor. 'Send it back for more.'

Cloudier had finally managed to find Clamdigger, and after an awkward greeting, had told him all about Fishbane and what she had read in 'The BeheMoths, and How We Frightened Them Away'. Clamdigger had, to his eternal credit in Cloudier's eyes, not doubted her for a moment, or patronised her, or asked her to repeat herself. He had simply jumped to the task, pulling as many people together as he could to help him.

They had gone to the place on the larboard side of the main deck, where a huge rope and pulley system stood, with two great wood and leather buckets swinging from a gibbet over a closed hatch. This was the water gurney – beneath the hatch was one of the Galloon's many reservoirs, which filled up in any storm, and which held water that was used for swabbing the decks and so on.

It was short work to organise the people they had mustered into a bucket chain, and to bring up the two buckets in quick succession, slopping over with chilly water. The buckets were big, each holding as much as a couple of bathtubs, so the harder part of the operation was to manhandle them off the pulley hooks, and over to where the nearest BeheMoths were at work.

As the makeshift detail was doing this sweaty work, Abel stood back a few feet, watching sceptically. As the first bucket had come up, he had said a few helpful things like, 'If this works, I'll be in the Captain's good books for sure!' but had otherwise done nothing to help.

Bucket One had done nothing to deter a particularly mean-looking BeheMoth from chewing up and swallowing the flag of Eisberg, which sat ready on deck to be used on the Galloon's arrival. Bucket Two had barely been noticed by a pair of moths that had begun chewing on the ropes of the water gurney itself. Now they were landing thick and fast, and Abel was nowhere to be seen.

Clamdigger was running back and forth, being organised and positive, but Cloudier could see that it was useless. Her research had failed. The one thing she felt sure would work made no difference at all. She chewed her lip and berated herself for thinking she was going to save the day. Clamdigger stopped congratulating the bucket chain on their efforts, and came over to her. She was mortified to see an element of pity in the look he gave her.

'I thought it was going to work for sure,' he said.

'I don't understand,' said Cloudier, and a prickle in her eyes told her she would have to work hard not to shed a tear of frustration. 'I thought the rainstorm frightened them off.'

'The Captain will think of something, Clouds,' said

Clamdigger, and his arm waggled clumsily as if he was wondering where to put it. 'Or maybe even Abel will.'

This made Cloudier look up and scour the deck for Skyman Abel. All she saw was the work detail returning to the business of fighting off the BeheMoths in any way they could.

'Where has Abel gone?' she asked.

After explaining the whole situation to the Bilgepump Orchestra a second time, Stanley was surprised that they were still not keen to stop their rehearsals, or to come up on deck and introduce themselves to the Captain.

'I'm sure he knows you're here anyway,' Stanley said. 'He's got spies everywhere.'

At this, a hurdy-gurdy player coughed guiltily and whispered something into the collar of his shirt, but Stanley wrote this off as a coincidence. He was just about to make an attempt to appeal to Mr Lungren's conscience, when beside him he saw Rasmussen draw herself up to her full height and adopt the facial expression she used when she was giving someone a good ticking off.

'Now, look here,' she said, and Stanley grimaced. This was the seventh worst of the nine possible openings to a Rasmussen ticking off, just below, 'It seems clear to me.' The orchestra, already feeling a bit sheepish, were all now fiddling with their tuning pegs, grinding their toes into the floor and generally trying hard to look as if they were somewhere else. But something strange happened. Rasmussen stopped before she had properly started. Stanley looked at her, and saw that she was no longer with them. She was staring into space, with her head cocked slightly on one side.

'Rasmussen?' he said tentatively.

She took him by the arm, and Mr Lungren by another, and without a word, started to walk.

'Erm. It's best just to go along when she does stuff like this,' said Stanley to Mr Lungren, who was looking alarmed, but was trotting along unresistingly.

'Where is she taking us?' he said. 'There's nothing through here but the cloakroom.'

They were trotting past the orchestra, across the dusty dancefloor, to a small door in the side wall of the ballroom. Rasmussen still had her head cocked, as if listening, but as she walked, she began bending her knees in an odd way, as if testing a trampoline she didn't trust.

'Back in a minute,' she called over her shoulder, and Stanley heard a murmur arise from the orchestra.

She pushed open the door with one foot, and led Mr Lungren and Stanley through to a room that was more brightly lit than the one they had left, although much, much smaller. There were rows of pegs along each wall, and at the far end, only fifteen feet or so from them, was a small lattice window. It was round like a porthole, and slightly too high up to be comfortable for any of them to look through.

Rasmussen stood in front of it, facing the wall still with her head to one side. Then she tipped it back the other way, and did the bouncing thing again. Instinctively, Mr Lungren and Stanley did it too, though neither of them knew why. But Stanley felt something odd.

'Something odd is happening,' she said.

'Well,' said Stanley, unsure of where to begin.

'Odder than usual, I mean,' she added, before he could start. 'Something is . . .'

'Attacking the Galloon,' said Stanley, and then wondered why he had said it.

Stanley had noticed that, sometimes, the people who loved the Galloon the most seemed to have a kind of sixth sense about it. The Captain, of course, knew every move it made whether he was at the wheel, asleep in his cot, or hanging off the prow chatting to Claude, the figurehead. Clamdigger sometimes knew when a rope had snapped, or a sail come loose, just by the creaking and tension in the woodwork, or a change in the way air flowed over the deck. Now Stanley got a sense of it too. It wasn't that he could physically feel a difference, not consciously anyway. He just knew the Galloon was in trouble.

'Upsy,' he said, and made a step out of his hands for Rasmussen to stand on. She stepped up, and looked out of the window. Silently she stepped down again, and they swapped over. Stanley looked out, saw what was going on, and also stepped down. He indicated to Mr Lungren to do the same.

Uncertainly, but seeming to understand that something important was happening, Mr Lungren stepped up into Rasmussen's hands, and put his other foot on Stanley's shoulder. He heaved himself up with slightly more fuss than was necessary, and then shrieked like a monkey on a rollercoaster. He clutched the window-sill, and screamed, wide-eyed, for a good long time. Then he fell backwards off his perch, his hands still clawed as if clutching the woodwork, even as he lay on his back on the ground.

'The Moths! The terrible Moths!' he gibbered. 'Something must be done! The Galloon needs our help!'

'Just what we thought,' said Stanley, as behind them, the bloodchilling features of a BeheMoth peered in through the little porthole.

On the deck of the Great Galloon, chaos still reigned. Able Skyman Abel was back and now he was marching backwards and forwards shouting orders, but not particularly useful ones, such as, 'Attack at dawn!' and 'Make another bucket chain!' Clamdigger was being slightly more helpful, rallying people and seeming to be everywhere at once.

Cook was boiling up a heartening stew, stopping occasionally to fling a well-aimed spud from his ladle. Mr and Mrs Wouldbegood were handing things out from the Galloon's depleted weapons store – a broken catapult, some hoes and a sharpened mop – and Ms Huntley, who had left the wheel room to help out at the front line, was trying to explain to the frightened crew what was going on.

'They won't hurt you directly!' she was shouting. 'And they mean us no harm! We'll just end up floating on the sea, with no means of propulsion.'

'Great!' yelped a woman at the back of the crowd. 'That's all we need!'

'Is it? Phew!' replied another voice. 'I thought we were in danger.'

There was a nervous laugh from everyone, unsure whether this was a joke or a mistake.

'We *are* in danger!' said Clamdigger, irritated that no one seemed to be taking this threat seriously. 'They will cling on to the balloon, sails and rigging, until they have eaten every last thread, or we plunge into the ocean, whichever happens first. We thought that water would scare them off, but it seems we are wrong. So we must continue to do everything we can to scare them away, or to shake them off. More are coming.'

'More! What can we do?' said Abel, forgetting himself momentarily.

'I heard they're not scared of anything,' shouted a woman holding a small child.

'It is true that they are not easy to scare, but we must do what we can,' said Clamdigger.

'I'm sorry,' said Cloudier dejectedly. 'I felt sure the rainstorm was significant somehow. I'll carry on reading up about them, see what else I can learn.'

'Reading! Pah! Who ever learned anything useful by reading? Where's the Captain when we need him?' said the woman again, causing a restless murmur amongst the crew and passengers, most of whom were now gathered on deck.

Suddenly the great bell clanged angrily.

'I am here,' said the Captain, and his voice carried easily over the crowd, with no obvious effort on his part. 'I appreciate that this is a terrifying situation, but every last one of you is here at your own risk. Something fundamental is wrong; quite besides these magnificent beasts taking a liking to my vessel, we are losing height. I have my suspicions as to why this may be, but have had many important things to think about.'

'His lost love,' whispered Cook emphatically, to a chorus of *sshh*.

'In a short while,' the Captain continued, 'I will ask Skyman Abel and his team to man the control ropes, and we will drift slowly to the surface of the sea, where the Galloon will function perfectly as a ship. Hopefully we will land before the BeheMoths do enough damage to cause us to plummet from the skies. On the water we may buy ourselves enough time to fight off the beasts. I cannot guarantee this.'

The woman who was holding a small child caught her breath, and the child began to sob.

'Those of you who wish to may use the life balloons to escape the ship, but be aware that they too will be seen by the BeheMoths as food. Those of you who wish to stay, listen to me. I have been thinking about what Cloudier Peele has told us, and I have a plan. If we work together, we may have one chance to keep the Galloon in the air, before we are forced to ditch. But I can make no promises.'

This was more than anyone on the ship had heard the Captain say in one go for weeks. He very rarely troubled himself now with the day-to-day goings-on onboard. His speech had the effect of focusing people's attention, and, instead of a rowdy mob, it was a disciplined crew that stood and waited for his orders.

'Stanley!' cried Ramalan down in the deeps of the Galloon, as Stanley and Rasmussen stood slightly apart, waiting for the result of the orchestra's pow-wow. 'Rasmussen!

The orchestra have decided to head up. We're going to help the Captain and let him know that we've been stowing away on his wonderful vessel. And I'd like to say thank you for finding my mouthpiece.' He held up the small brass thing Stanley had found. 'Now the Boomaphone will sound much nicer.'

'Although just as loud,' said Mr Lungren, who was recovering his composure slightly, and had been explaining the situation to them.

'When we do get back on deck, I would like to apologise to everyone for the loud noises,' said Mr Ramalan. 'I didn't realise I was causing so much trouble.'

'It's really quite alright. It's a, er, unique instrument,' said Stanley, as tactfully as he could manage, while looking around for any chandelier that looked like it might conceal a quick way back onto the deck.

'But there're more important things going on.' Rasmussen was hopping up and down with impatience. 'The Galloon is being attacked by terrible creatures! We have to get on deck and help fight them off.'

The members of the orchestra began murmuring amongst themselves.

'Terrible creatures?' piped up a minuscule piccolo player. 'These little insect things?'

'I couldn't quite do them justice,' said Mr Lungren sheepishly.

Stanley took a deep breath. 'They're huge, terrifying,

skellington-faced butterfly-looking dust-flappers!' he said portentously.

'BeheMoths!' cried Rasmussen.

The hubbub of noise died down. The members of the orchestra looked at each other, wide-eyed.

'BeheMoths, eh?' said Ramalan, and he cracked his many knuckles. 'Perhaps we'd better get up there and have a look at 'em.'

'BeheMoths, yes,' said Stanley. 'I wasn't sure you'd know what that was.'

Rasmussen grinned from ear to ear.

And with that, the whole orchestra gave a whoop that sounded more than slightly like a war cry. As one, they all turned to their instruments and began adjusting, unscrewing, destringing and reconfiguring the strange assortment of contraptions. Soon a pattern began to emerge. Stanley saw that the cellists were now carrying things that looked more like mahogany crossbows, with bows loaded where bolts would be.

The piccolo player dropped a dart down the end of his instrument, and with a puff of the cheeks sent it ricocheting off a tuba. All around them, instruments of music were becoming weapons of war. The drums began to roll, and then set up a slow, ominous beat. As one being, the orchestra began to move at a jogging pace along the corridor. Mr Ramalan picked up Stanley in one great hand, and Rasmussen in the other.

With the third he helped a company of violin archers pick up the Boomaphone.

'It is many a long age since the orchestra went to war!' he shouted over the racket.

'This is exciting, isn't it?' said Rasmussen to Stanley.

'Yes,' said Stanley. 'Almost as exciting as an adventure!'

'Starboard, thirty degrees – that is, right a bit!' yelled the Captain up on deck, and the team of burly men manning the great iron harpoon gun spun wheels, pulled levers, and aimed at the nearest BeheMoth, flying alongside.

'FIRE!' ordered the Captain, calmly but with great force.

The eight-foot-long iron harpoon whistled out of the mouth of its cannon. Clamdigger heard it slice through the air, and smelt the rope burning as it uncoiled at great speed.

'MISS!' shouted the Captain. 'Haul her in and try again!' and the team began to haul on the rope, ready for another shot.

The BeheMoths were upon them. They looked like a diabolical cross between a death's-head moth and a cockroach of incredible size. Their antennae flickered as they flew alongside the Galloon, sniffing out food wherever they could find it.

'Fire again when ready, men!' the Captain said to the harpoon crew.

'Sir?' said a voice at his elbow.

'Yes, Abel?' snapped the Captain, gruffly.

'Will this work, sir?' Abel was plucking at imaginary fluff on his lapel.

'We may pick off a couple of the beasts,' said the Captain, watching intently as a harpoon careered wildly off into the sky. 'And it'll give us time.'

'Time for what sir?'

'Time,' said Captain Anstruther, 'for Plan B. I believe Cloudier was quite right about the thunderstorm being crucial to scaring off the BeheMoths. But it wasn't the rain that did it.'

He pointed at the crowd that was reassembling on the deck, each individual carrying pots, pans, drums and sticks.

'I believe,' he said, 'that the BeheMoths are extremely sensitive to noise. I do not know if we can make enough noise to drive off this many. But we must do our best. It may only give us time to land safely, but if that is the case then so be it.'

At that point another phalanx of BeheMoths made it through the flurry of harpoons and landed on the foremast jib b'loon. Their awful faces seemed to be mocking the crew as they bit into the heavy canvas, and everybody could hear the crunching noises they made.

'They are upon us in ever greater numbers,' cried

the Captain, as yet more of the beasts landed all around him. 'To arms!' And with that he began ringing the great ship's bell as if every life on the Great Galloon relied upon it, which, of course, it did.

The Brunt sat up on the edge of his bed. The last rounds of noise had really taken it out of him. He looked pale and relatively weak. But he had in his ears the large pair of wax earplugs that Mr Lungren had given him at Rasmussen's request. He was drinking a large mug of tea that Stanley had made before returning to the daylight, braving the furnace as a favour to his new friend.

The Brunt yawned and stretched. He took a big gulp of tea, then stood up with a look of determination in his eyes. He grabbed his enormous shovel from where it leaned against the wall and made his way down the corridor to the furnace room.

He had some stoking to do.

The orchestra came at last, with Stanley and Rasmussen's help, to the area below the platform from which they had taken their tumble. Far, far above they could see a tiny rectangle of light, and Stanley was horrified to see the occasional dark shape flit past.

'The BeheMoths!' he said. 'We must help. The Captain needs us!'

'How did you get down here?' asked Mr Lungren politely, but Rasmussen's reply was not so well mannered.

'We fell!' she snapped. 'And as far as I know we can't fall back up again, and there's no other way of getting out of here because it's normally the Brunt who does it and he's . . . he's . . .'

'He's here,' said Stanley simply.

He was indeed. Like an avalanche on Carpet Mountain, the Brunt was lumbering out of the gloom towards them. Neither Stanley nor Rasmussen had seen him from a distance yet, and somehow he looked even bigger in this open space than he did in his cosy little room. His horns curled magnificently way over his head, so the orchestra members had to lean right back to take him all in, even while he was a fair way off.

As he approached, he reached out a thickly furred arm and grabbed hold of a large wooden beam that lay unnoticed in the darkness. He dragged this along with him as he came, and the noise was almost as unnerving as the Boomaphone.

For a fleeting second, Stanley wondered whether a happy, headache-free Brunt would be as sympathetic as he had been earlier. But he needn't have worried.

Despite the quailing knees and quiet moans of the Bilgepump Orchestra, the Brunt meant them no harm. He stopped just in front of them and spoke, in his alarmingly quiet way.

'Hello, Stanley.'

He seemed to be waiting. Stanley felt Rasmussen's nudge and replied.

'Hello, the Brunt.'

'Hello, Rasmussen,' said the Brunt.

'Hello, the Brunt.'

Stanley was relieved that the Brunt didn't know the names of all the orchestra members, or they would have run out of time to help save the ship.

'Ermm. What have you got there?' asked Rasmussen, referring to the beam the Brunt had hauled behind him, and the apparatus it was attached to.

The Brunt looked at it slowly, then turned back to them, a beam of his own spreading slowly across his wide, leathery face.

'It's a spare platform, Rasmussen,' he said. 'I can pull you up onto the deck, like flour or potatoes.'

Stanley laughed out loud.

As his head rose above the parapet at the end of the long, precarious journey to the outside, Stanley saw swarms of gigantic creatures clinging to the rigging, the balloons, the sails and every surface, munching and crunching, blind to the panic all around them. He also saw the entire crew of the Galloon standing in clumps, being directed by Clamdigger, Cloudier, and a few other trustworthy types. They were all banging on pots and

149

pans, blowing into kettles, shouting, and ringing bells as loudly as they could.

'What's going on?' he shouted to Mr Wouldbegood, who tutted and adjusted his cap disapprovingly. 'Band practice?'

As they clambered off the rickety platform and onto the deck, Mr Wouldbegood told the assembled orchestra, Stanley and Rasmussen about Captain Anstruther's Plan B, with particular reference to how it wouldn't have come to this in his day, and how a spell in the army would do these BeheMoths some good.

Once everyone was safe, Rasmussen leaned over the hatchway and cupped her hands round her mouth.

'Thank you, the Brunt!' she yelled.

No reply was heard, but a couple of seconds later the platform gave a kind of shimmy, as if the Brunt was waggling his rope in recognition.

As Stanley turned away from the hatch, Mrs Wouldbegood was still complaining under her breath. 'So we're supposed to make a lot of noise to scare these ruddy creatures off the rigging and so on, but I don't think we're going to get anywhere with these little pots and pans. We need something that can make a *real* noise, like in the olden days.'

Stanley turned to Rasmussen, and then they both looked at Mr Ramalan.

'A real noise, eh?' the three of them said together.

150

A few minutes later, the orchestra was assembled around the main mast, where only metres above their heads, a thick carpet of BeheMoths was busy chewing through the sail.

'I appreciate the gesture, Miss Rasmussen, Stanley, but is a chamber concert really the best way to deal with this crisis?' said Able Skyman Abel, from the back of a terrified crowd.

'It's exactly what's needed, Skyman Abel,' said Stanley, giving out the last of the spare earplugs that the orchestra had provided. 'You'll particularly enjoy the finale, I believe!'

'Mr Lungren, proceed,' said Rasmussen.

'What?' said Mr Lungren.

Rasmussen held up another delicately handwritten cardboard notice, which this time said:

Pray, Begin

The conductor nodded seriously, and with a glance at the BeheMoths above his head, raised his keep-in-time stick.

With the earplugs in, Rasmussen and Stanley were astonished at the difference in the orchestra's sound. Where before they had heard discordant clanging, grating and sawing noises, now they heard the gentle rise and fall of a beautiful symphony as it played around the decks. And as they played, each member of the orchestra

151

still wielded his or her instrument as a weapon. The violinists, each with a quiver of bows at his thigh, were firing into the crowd of Behemoths with every pizzicato note. The timpanist was bashing away with his beaters at more than just his drums, and the double bass player was holding his instrument like a gigantic club, all the while keeping up a driving backbeat. And at the back was Mr Ramalan, all three arms once more engaged in readying the Boomaphone for its moment. The crew stood in awe, including the Captain on the bridge, and even the BeheMoths that weren't directly under fire stopped chomping and raised their antennae.

The music went on for quite a while, building to a peak here, and then falling back to a gentle tune on one instrument, before rising on a stirring crescendo once again. The assembled people even forgot for a while that they were being attacked by all-consuming monster moths, such was the beauty of it. Any BeheMoth that got too close was picked off, but overall the assault continued. Somehow, though, the Gallooniers knew that something big was about to happen.

Clamdigger and Cloudier stood together, manifestly not holding hands. And then Stanley noticed Mr Ramalan cracking his knuckles, adjusting his position and inflating his cheeks at the mouthpiece of the Boomaphone. A thrill went through him, as he realised that he was going to listen to the noise again, this time on purpose. He hoped it worked, but if it didn't, what did it matter?

The Gallooniers had long ago stopped panicking, and the banging on pans was never going to work anyway. The music swelled yet further, and Mr Lungren was standing on tiptoes as he worked up to the Grand Finale. Stanley looked round at the crowd, and felt very proud and pleased to be a part of it.

Mr Ramalan took an almighty breath, flexed the muscles in all three of his arms, applied them to the relevant pedals, flaps and valves and blew for all he was worth. With the earplugs in, and the new mouth-piece, the sound that reached Stanley's brain was a fat, warm, chocolaty tone that made him feel safe and happy. It still rumbled up through his belly and made his eyes shake; it still set the Galloon shuddering like a tumble dryer, but it was such a satisfyingly cheerful feeling that he couldn't help laughing.

Stanley grabbed Rasmussen's arm and pointed upwards – the balloon was jiggling like a jelly again, and the BeheMoths couldn't stand it. They were drop-ping off in swathes, flapping their enormous wings, and flying silently away from the Great Galloon.

Looking around, he saw people laughing and shouting, although obviously he couldn't hear them, and he even caught a glimpse of the Captain's face under his imposing hat. He thought that maybe he detected the beginnings of a smile there, the closest he had seen the Captain get to a true show of happiness since his ill-fated wedding day.

The orchestra carried on playing as the BeheMoths flapped away, but soon their music became a jaunty hornpipe, and around Stanley the crew of the Galloon were tidying up and assessing the damage while jigging and reeling about the decks in a ceilidh of triumph. Stanley watched as Clamdigger and Cloudier each picked up one end of a small sail that had fallen to the deck, and folded them into the middle, where they met with a sheepish roll of the eyes. Ms Huntley tapped Cloudier on the shoulder.

'You could ask Mr Clamdigger to our rooms for tea, if you like,' she said brightly.

'Muum!' wailed Cloudier, with the diphthong that only a thirteen-year-old girl can pronounce.

'Just a thought!' replied her mother, wheeling away as a deckhand took her by the arm.

Rasmussen joined Stanley, and they watched as Cloudier looked up again at the cabin boy.

'Four o'clock tomorrow, then? I'll make a cake.' Then she added huffily, 'I suppose you've got "duties", though,' and looked at her nails.

'No, I suppose I can,' said Clamdigger. 'I think Abel owes me an afternoon off.' And as he turned away from

Cloudier with the sail in his arms, Stanley saw a smile spread across each of their faces, unbeknown to the other.

'Great,' said Rasmussen. 'I expect we'll get invited for cake too.'

'Ermm,' Stanley began, but the clanging of the great wheelhouse bell saved him from having to let her down gently. They turned to see the Captain standing on the rail of the quarter deck, waving his second-best hat above his head.

'People of the Great Galloon!' he called, and as ever his voice carried above the wind and hubbub in a way that seemed almost magical. 'I owe you much. I owe you my life, for those beasts would surely have sunk the Galloon if you were not so brave and hearty. I owe you my loyalty, for you have shown loyalty to me that I scarcely deserve. And I owe you an apology.'

At this, the crowd, which was thickening now around Stanley and Rasmussen, set up a chorus of dissent. 'No!' they cried, and, 'You owe us nothing of the sort.'

'You are kind,' continued the Captain. 'But you are wrong. I have been too long in a brown study, leaving the running of my beloved Galloon to others, however *able* they may be. I should never have left it to Cloudier to warn us of the approaching BeheMoths, or of the Galloon's unscheduled descent. But warn us she did, and we are grateful.'

At this, Cloudier went red and examined her nails minutely, but her mother gave her a hefty squeeze, and a smattering of applause ran round those near her.

'It should not have been up to Clamdigger to bring me her message. Or Stanley and Rasmussen to investigate the worrisome noises. But it was, and I am as proud of them as I am ashamed of myself.'

'No!' called Rasmussen, and a few others took up the cry.

'Yes,' continued Captain Anstruther. 'And as for my self-appointed second in command, Able Skyman Abel . . .'

Stanley craned his neck and saw, a few hundred feet away, Abel begin to step gingerly backwards down a hatchway, as if hoping no one would see him.

'If he had not convinced you all that I was the real Meredith Anstruther, all those weeks ago, then I would have had a real struggle on my hands.'

Abel stopped creeping away, and waved at the crowd, beaming with relief.

'Hmmmm,' said Rasmussen, through tight lips.

'Quite so,' agreed Stanley.

'So I hope you can forgive me . . .' said the Captain, to cries of "yes", and "nothing to forgive you for!", '. . . and join me in this: a rousing three cheers, for the crew of the Great Galloon! Hip hip!'

'Hooray!' cried the crew, most of whom were now

156

trying to squeeze into the space in front of the wheel-house, where Stanley stood.

'Hooray!' they cried again at the Captain's instigation, and many threw their hats, walking sticks, instruments or children in the air.

'HOORAY!' they finished, and everyone hugged and backslapped like it was Hogmanay. But in the middle of the throng, Stanley, while being lifted into the air by an enthusiastic grown-up, took the time to look around him. He saw Ms Huntley, staring up at the Captain with a wistful look in her eye. He saw the Countess, radiating beauty and elegantly dancing with Cook. He saw the Wouldbegoods, Rasmussen and many hundreds more, smiling, dancing and cheering with joy. And he saw the Captain, scanning the horizon, already lost once more in the search for his kidnapped bride.

A day or so after the BeheMoth escape, Stanley and Rasmussen were called to the Captain's office, with its green leather-topped table, and its smell of brass polish and toasted cheese.

They explained all about meeting the Brunt, finding the orchestra and all that had happened to them down below.

'But we'd really like to go back down, sir, to check that the Brunt is alright,' said Rasmussen, at the end of her long and breathless explanation.

'You may certainly visit the Brunt whenever you like, although if I know him, he won't want to be disturbed *too* often. However, if it's proof of his wellbeing you're after, look up there.' And, turning them round, he pointed through the window at the huge main chimney-funnel of the Great Galloon. They were pleased to see that it was once again belching out clouds of black smoke, as it had always done before, when they took it entirely for granted.

'The Brunt is stoking the fire!' said Stanley.

'Yes, he is, which means we're rising again, and we'll make our rendezvous at the Eisberg Mountains in time for the Count's birthday celebrations.'

'I don't think we should invite the Brunt to the celebration concert, though,' said Rasmussen.

'And where will we go after that sir?' said Stanley, pushing his luck in this moment of solidarity. The Captain was quiet, and his eyes flicked towards the mantelpiece where a small portrait of a beautiful, upright young woman stood.

'I have an appointment in the Chimney Isles,' he said, with the sadness once again returning to his steel-grey eyes. 'With my brother, although he will be surprised to see me, no doubt.'

He seemed to drift away for a moment, then snap back into the present.

'Now, you will recall that you had been volunteered

to tidy the hold, scrub the decks and keep watch until we got to Eisberg. I think in view of recent events, you can be excused these duties.' The two friends punched the air. 'I believe, however, that you were waiting for an adventure to happen, and I would hate for you to miss it. So for now, you are excused.'

'Yes, sir,' said Stanley and Rasmussen together, and they turned towards the door. Before he closed it, Stanley looked at the Captain again, bent over his map table, studying it hard with his pipe clamped tightly between his teeth.

'And, sir?' he said quietly.

'Yes, Stanley?'

'Good luck, sir.'

'Thank you, Stanley. That will be all.'

Honorary Galloonier's aptitude test with Able Skyman Abel

Those testees who score 100% or more qualify as honorary Gallooniers, and may refer to themselves as such at parties. Pop to the Captain's Cabin for hot chocolate and a hearty pat on the back.

Those who score 99% or less, head to your nearest long-distance examinator for further lessons from Mrs Crumplehorn. Or turn the page to find the answers. The test may be taken once, more than once, or more than more than once, as the testee sees fit. Pencils at the ready please.

You may turn over your papers now.

Q1. What is the correct term for the front end of a craft such as the Great Galloon?

a) The bow
b) The stern
c) Able Skyman Abel
d) The pointy bit

Q2. Who owns the most impressive hat on board the Great Galloon?

a) Captain Meredith Anstruther
b) Able Skyman Abel
c) Second Leftenant 'Ten Gallon' Twistleton
d) Bonny, the giant baby

Q3. What is the first name of the troublesome and uncouth child known as 'Rasmussen'?

a) Cloth ears
b) Little Miss Fancypants
c) Mary, or Anna, or Marianna, or something
d) Able Skyman Abel

Q4. What is the correct way to address the Dowager Countess of Hammerstein?

a) Oi, mush!
b) Able Skyman Abel
c) May it please your inscrutable mellifluence . . .
d) Any way you like, she's very nice and doesn't mind

Q5. Why is that small irritating chap, Sidney Crinklestain or whatever, so furry?

   a) Because his Great Aunt Dotty was an otter
   b) Because he's no better than he ought to be
   c) Nobody knows
   d) Able Skyman Abel

Q6. During the affair of the unfeasibly loud noises, who saved the Galloon from all-devouring monster moths?

   a) Stinky Crumbleton and Rasputin, or whatever they're called
   b) Mr Lungren and his Bilgepump Orchestra
   c) The entire crew of the Galloon, working together
   d) Able Skyman Abel

Q7. On the Galloon, who drinks more cups of tea per day?

   a) Cook
   b) The Brunt
   c) Cloudier Peele
   d) Able Skyman Abel

Q8. When onboard a vessel such as the Galloon, where does one go to the lavatory?

   a) The heads
   b) The poop deck
   c) Over the side and hope for the best
   d) Able Skyman Abel

Q9. If Cloudier Peele had two slices of cake, but gave one away and ate half of the other one, and Clamdigger had three slices of cake, ate one and a half of them but didn't give any away, who would have the most cake?

a) Clamdigger
b) Cloudier
c) They would have the same
d) Able Skyman Abel

Q10. If you were sitting at a desk in your study on a middle deck of the Galloon, slightly for'ard of the mainmast, near the butler's pantry, what would be the quickest way to get to the mess in time for dinner?

a) Down two decks, hop on a trolleybus heading amidships, hop off before the last stop, duck through Manly's department store, and ride the moving staircase up to the mess

b) A brisk walk hard towards the stern for twenty minutes, then jog down beggars alley, over the wooden bridge by the *Octopus Arms* and you're there

c) I'm not sure but I hope you know because I'm famished

d) No, really. How do I get to the mess? I've clean forgotten and it must be teatime soon. Clamdigger? CLAMDI– oh, there you are boy. Chop chop . . . now . . . I wonder what's for pudding tonight?

ANSWERS:

Anyone who answered 'Able Skyman Abel' to every question has learned that, of course, the best way to become an honorary Galloonier is to stay on the right side of me. Full marks. Everyone else report to –

> *Now now Abel, you've had your fun. Mark it properly, there's a good man.*

> Of course, Captain, I was always going to ... erm. Right. Here goes.

Q1. a). The bow is the front end of a ship or similar craft. Pointy bit also acceptable. The stern is the rear end. By which I don't mean the bottom. Calm down.

Q2. a). While my own hat is impressive in its own subtle way, the Captain's hat is of course, quite a marvel of modern millinery. His very best hat is currently gracing the head of his dastardly brother somewhere under the seven seas, but even his second-best hat is quite a thing to behold.

Q3. I'm sure it's c). Miranda, Montana, something like that. Starts with an M anyway. Or a K. Pete? No, it's not Pete. Definitely a girly name.

Q4. The Dowager Countess of Hammerstein is possessed of boundless grace and infinite understanding. Any polite form of address is acceptable. Therefore the correct answer is c).

Q5. c). Nobody knows. Not even him, apparently. Very odd.

Q6. d). Well, alright, c). But that includes me.

Q7. Cook spends all day making tea, but rarely drinks it. Cloudier Peele wants everyone to think she prefers those mimsy 'teas' made of rosehips and cloudberries and hummingbird tears or what have you, although I happen to know she drinks builder's tea with milk and two when no one's looking. I have the odd cuppa, but I think the Brunt must win out here. So it's b).

Q8. a). On vessels such as this, and more conventional ocean-going ships, the toilets are called the 'heads'. So full marks for that answer. Over the side is never acceptable, as I found out to my cost when . . . never mind.

Q9. d). In any situation where Cloudier and Clamdigger each had cake, I would end up with the most cake. These youngsters need to learn a thing or two about sharing.

Q10. d) again. And for those of you who are interested, it was rhubarb crumble and custard.